Presents

Take a look at our books for September!

A marriage ended or a marriage mended? Kayla has been bought back by her estranged husband, billionaire Duardo Alvarez, in Helen Bianchin's scorcher *Purchased by the Billionaire*. Bedded for revenge or wedded for passion? Freya has made the mistake of hiding the existence of Italian Enrico Ranieri's little son, and she must make amends as his convenient wife in Michelle Reid's torrid tale *The Ranieri Bride*. Is revenge sweet? Greek tycoon Christos Carides certainly thinks so when he seduces Becca Summer in Kim Lawrence's sizzling story, *The Carides Pregnancy*. But for how long? Out for the count? Italian aristocrat Alessio Ramontella certainly thinks he's KO'd innocent English beauty Laura, but will she actually succumb to his ruthless seduction? Find out in *The Count's Blackmail Bargain* by Sara Craven. Meantime, Carol Marinelli's mixing business with intense pleasure in her new UNCUT novel, *Taken for His Pleasure*. It's a gold band of blackmail for temporary bride Maddison as she's forced to marry wealthy Greek Demetrius Papasakis in *The Greek's Convenient Wife* by Melanie Milburne. Mistress material? Nora Lang doesn't think she's got what it takes in Susan Napier's *Mistress for a Weekend*. But tycoon Blake MacLeod thinks Nora definitely has something special—confidential information. And he'll keep her in his bed to prevent her giving it away. Finally, an ultimatum...*The Marriage Ultimatum* by Helen Brooks. It's Carter Blake's only option when Liberty refuses to let him take her.

Carol Marinelli

Taken for His
Pleasure

uNcut

TORONTO • NEW YORK • LONDON
AMSTERDAM • PARIS • SYDNEY • HAMBURG
STOCKHOLM • ATHENS • TOKYO • MILAN • MADRID
PRAGUE • WARSAW • BUDAPEST • AUCKLAND

ISBN-13: 978-0-373-12566-1
ISBN-10:   0-373-12566-6

TAKEN FOR HIS PLEASURE

First North American Publication 2006.

Copyright © 2006 by The SAL Marinelli Family Trust.

www.eHarlequin.com

Printed in U.S.A.

All about the author...
Carol Marinelli

CAROL MARINELLI finds writing a bio rather like writing her New Year's resolutions. Oh, she'd love to say that since she wrote the last one, she now goes to the gym regularly and doesn't stop for coffee, cake and gossip afterward; that she's incredibly organized, and that she writes for a few productive hours a day after tidying her immaculate house and taking a brisk walk with the dog.

The reality is Carol spends an inordinate amount of time daydreaming about dark, brooding men and exotic places (research), which doesn't leave too much time for the gym, housework or anything that comes in between. And her most productive writing hours happen to be in the middle of the night, which leaves her in a constant state of bewildered exhaustion.

Originally from England, Carol now lives in Melbourne, Australia. She adores going back to the U.K. for a visit—actually, she adores going anywhere for a visit—and constantly (expensively) strives to overcome her fear of flying. She has three gorgeous children who are growing up so fast (too fast—they've just worked out that she lies about her age!) and keep her busy with a never-ending round of homework, sports and friends coming over.

A nurse and a writer, Carol writes for the Harlequin Presents and Medical Romance lines, and is passionate about both. She loves the fast-paced, busy setting of a modern hospital, but every now and then admits it's bliss to escape to the glamorous, alluring world of her heroes and heroines in Harlequin Presents novels. A bit like her real life actually!

CHAPTER ONE

'LUCKY YOU!' Maria shouted, holding the punch bag as Lydia boxed away, repeating the words like some kind of chant as Lydia thumped ever harder.

Lydia's red curls had long since worked their way out of her hair tie, and moved in time as she pounded the punch bag, her pale, slender arms delivering surprisingly strong blows. The rhythmic, vigorous exercise was wonderfully cathartic as, egged on by Maria, Lydia vented some of her anger and frustration.

'Lucky, lucky you! Come on, Lydia. Hit harder!'

'I'm done!' Lydia breathed, shaking her head and resting her gloved hands on her knees. 'And *lucky* certainly isn't how I'd describe myself, being stuck here for the next few nights—I haven't had a day off for weeks!'

Even though the place was deserted, mindful that someone could be listening, Lydia spoke in low tones as she pulled off her gloves and turned the sink taps on full blast to distort their conversation. She needlessly refilled her water bottle and took a few moments to splash her face.

'What are you moaning about? Being joined at the hip with Anton Santini is my idea of an absolute dream job. Imagine how I feel!' Maria grinned, offering Lydia her own water bottle to fill. 'Being lumbered playing assistant to his female PA! Why couldn't they have given *me* Anton Santini to guard?'

Lydia held up a long strand of red curls in answer and gave a wry smile. 'I don't somehow think I'd make a very good undercover Italian PA, when the only Italian words I know are the names of pasta!'

'I'd go ginger in a moment if it meant sharing a bedroom with Anton Santini.' Maria giggled. 'I still can't believe they chose *you* to pass off as his girlfriend!'

If it had been anyone other than Maria saying it Lydia would have thought the comment sounded catty, but Maria was simply speaking the truth—it *was* unbelievable that she'd been considered the most suitable person to serve as Anton Santini's girlfriend during his whirlwind visit to Australia.

Anton Santini liked his women petite, stylishly groomed and demure.

Lydia was painfully aware that she failed on all three.

Although her body was slender and toned, she stood five feet eight without heels—five feet ten if her mass of red curls was running particularly wild! Lydia wore jeans and T-shirts like a second skin, and as for demure—well, it wasn't exactly a prerequisite for a detective. Sure, she refused to buy into the beer-swilling, coarse language world of some of her colleagues, but she wasn't exactly afraid of expressing an opinion...

'Smile, Lydia! You're a real misery this morning,' Maria observed. 'This is one of the top hotels in Melbourne, we've been given full access to everything, and here you are moaning...' Catching Lydia's frown,

Maria looked around and, seeing a yawning man stag-gering into the massive pool area outside the gymna-sium, abruptly ended the conversation.

'Fancy a sauna?' Maria asked, and Lydia was about to shake her head—a sauna was the absolute last thing she *fancied* at this hour of the morning—but she knew it was the one room in the place where it had been agreed detectives could meet and talk unhindered.

After rolling her eyes in protest, Lydia gave a very sweet, very false smile. 'What a great idea!'

'How's Angelina?' Lydia asked, once they were wrapped in white towels with the door safely closed.

'Efficient.' Maria rolled her eyes. 'And extremely talkative! I can't believe his entire team travels ahead of him to ensure that everything is to his liking!'

'It's just as well that they do,' Lydia pointed out. 'It's thanks to Angelina's efficiency that we're even aware of the security threat.'

'Yeah, but it's not much to go on though,' Maria mused. 'A bunch of flowers sent to his hotel room before his ar-rival—they could just be from an old girlfriend—'

'I doubt it,' Lydia interrupted. 'Given that on the two previous occasions Santini was sent flowers he was in-volved in potentially life-threatening incidents! It's a bit of a coincidence, don't you think? Not forgetting all the abusive phone calls Angelina's been fielding. It's right the Feds are taking this seriously. Can you just imagine the negative publicity if something happens to him?'

'I guess.' Maria shrugged. 'It just seems a bit over the top—senior detectives acting as bodyguards. They've even got Kevin behind the bar fixing drinks—it just seems so extreme.'

'If this deal Santini's looking to sign up goes ahead, then it's going to be such a massive boost for tourism. I'm not surprised that all the stops are being pulled out to protect him!'

Cheerfully ladling water onto the coals and upping the already stifling temperature several degrees, Maria, unlike Lydia, was only too happy to veer off the subject of work. 'I love it here,' she rattled on happily. 'We're going to look fabulous by the time this assignment's over—can you feel your pores unclogging?'

'I can feel my hair frizzing,' Lydia replied, sitting down on the bench. Tears were appallingly close, and she wished she could snap out of her morose mood, surprised at how much Maria's 'misery' comment had stung.

Burying her face in the towel for a moment, Lydia closed her eyes and dragged in the stifling air. 'I really wanted the next couple of nights off,' she carefully elaborated. 'I had things to do.'

'What could you possibly have to do?' Maria smiled, her words laced with friendly sarcasm. 'You know that a detective's not supposed to have a life.'

'I just wanted a couple of days to myself.' Lydia gave a defeated shrug. 'You know—listening to music, eating chocolate, feeling sorry for myself…'

Seeing her friend and colleague, usually so assured, so driven and focussed, slumped on a bench with her face hidden by a towel, Maria faded out the wisecracks, and sat down next to her, her voice gentle. 'What's going on, Lydia? Is it you and Graham?'

'We broke up.' Lydia nodded, finally peeking out from the towel and seeing Maria's shocked expression.

'But you two seemed so happy!'

'We were.' Lydia shrugged. 'So long as I didn't mention work.' She took a deep breath and, closing her eyes, shook her head. 'And with a job like ours it doesn't exactly leave much else to talk about. I thought Graham was different; I thought the fact we were both detectives meant that he'd understand that I wouldn't be greeting him at the door at the end of a long day all scented and oiled in a strappy little number…'

'Graham didn't want that from you.' Maria gave a shocked laugh. 'Lydia, he adored you—jeans and all!'

'I thought he did.' Lydia swallowed. 'But over the last few weeks he's been acting weird. When I was on that drug stake-out he kept ringing me up about the most ridiculous things—'

'He was worried,' Maria broke in. 'That was one hell of a dangerous job, Lydia. I was worried about you too!'

'But you didn't phone me on the hour every hour,' Lydia pointed out. 'You didn't ring me at two in the morning to ask if I needed someone to feed my goldfish.'

'Your goldfish died last year!'

'Exactly,' Lydia said dryly. 'And then we were going to his mum's for dinner one night and he asked me to dress up a bit…'

'Dress up?'

'It wasn't as if I was in jeans or a tracksuit for heaven's sake. I was wearing a black suit! And then he asked if maybe while we were at his mum's I could try to refrain from mentioning work…' Lydia paused as Maria's lips tightened, watching as her friend struggled to give an objective answer.

'Lydia, it *is* a dangerous job, and we do see a lot of the more seamy side of life—it must be hard for any man to put up with, let alone someone who knows the full truth about what we do. I know my father and brothers *hate* my job, and they don't know the half of it! I'm the family shame.' Maria nudged Lydia until finally she managed a glimmer of a smile. 'So, who finally finished it?'

'Me,' Lydia said, chewing on her bottom lip for a moment, not sure whether to reveal her secret—the supposedly good news that had finally brought things between her and Graham to a head. 'I'm being considered for a promotion.'

Maria's eyes widened and a smile broke out on her face. Because they really were good friends, as well as colleagues, and because they both knew how tough it could be to climb the ladder in what was still very much a man's profession, Maria's smile was completely genuine and her embrace was warm as she hugged her friend. 'Inspector Lydia Holmes.'

'It's not definite,' Lydia quickly pointed out. 'But Graham found out, and suddenly all the little niggles, all the little problems we'd been having lately, seemed to magnify.'

'Is he jealous?' Maria asked, and Lydia gave a soft, mirthless laugh.

'Apparently not! He insists that he's just worried about me. He says that he's not sure if it's the sort of job he wants his wife doing. He doesn't think—'

'Back up a second.' Maria was way too sharp to miss a snippet of conversation as juicy as this! 'So you've had an offer of promotion and a proposal?'

'An offer of promotion *or* a proposal,' Lydia corrected. 'It would seem I can't have both.'

'Oh, Lydia.' Maria's groan was sympathetic. The problem was all too usual—one that had been pondered by female detectives the world over. As attractive and as sexy as a kick butt detective might sound to a potential lover, the cruel reality was that she didn't make promising wife material. This didn't matter a scrap, of course—until you met someone you really cared about. 'What are you going to do?'

'I've already done it!' Lydia gave a firm nod as Maria winced. 'We really are finished.'

'Then let's just hope it was worth it. I mean with the promotion coming up and everything—let's just hope you get it.'

'It doesn't matter if I get it or not,' Lydia said firmly. 'It would be nice, but it just wasn't working out between me and Graham. If he can't take me as I am, then it wasn't meant to be.'

'Well, at least you get to lick your wounds in style!' Maria said. 'Full access to the beauty salon *and* you've been placed with Anton Santini—you're a single girl now, Lydia. Who better to have a rebound relationship with?'

'Anton Santini doesn't *do* relationships,' Lydia said, a smile finally wobbling on her face. She felt so much better for having opened up to her friend. She gave a tiny shocked laugh. 'You haven't read what I read last night—his bio's unbelievable! He's always been a bit of a rake, but this last year I swear the man's been on a mission! His list of ex-girlfriends reads like the top one hundred most beautiful people in the world: actresses, European royalty, supermodels, soccer-players' wives…'

'Who?' Maria asked, agog. 'Anyone I know?'

'Yep.' Lydia nodded, but didn't elaborate. 'And every last one has ended in tears—for the woman at least.'

'Is he really that bad?'

'Worse!' Lydia nodded. 'And I'm supposed to be guarding him. God, I hope he behaves himself.'

'Well, if he doesn't you can always pass him over to me—I'll entertain him for you!'

'You'd be so much better at this than me,' Lydia happily conceded. 'You're way more suited to Anton Santini.'

'I'm not sure if that's a compliment.' Maria feigned a hurt expression. 'If you're implying that just because I once had Botox…'

'I'm implying that you're a born flirt.' Lydia laughed. 'I'm implying that you're so gorgeous no one would turn a hair if *you* were draped over Santini's arm. Whereas I'm going to look so awkward and out of place tagging along beside him…'

'You'll be wonderful,' Maria wailed. 'You'll look fabulous and you're going to have an absolute ball. Unlike me. Angelina's well over sixty, a confirmed spinster, and tops the scales at one hundred kilos. You'd think someone as divine as Anton would hire a gorgeous assistant. I guess this one must help him keep his mind strictly on business…'

'You're shocking.' Lydia laughed again. 'This is supposed to be work, remember?'

'I know.' Maria managed a tiny groan, but it changed into a giggle as she stared down at the very new, very false nails she'd had applied the moment they'd checked into the hotel yesterday. 'Right, I'm really cooked now.' Maria stood up. 'And if we're going to pull this off, I suppose we ought to hit the beauty parlour. I've got to start looking like a chic Italian businesswoman, while you, Lydia Holmes…' Maria's voice trailed off as Lydia groaned. 'It will be fun,' Maria insisted. 'It's going to be like one of those makeovers on the television—watching you turn from a dark-suited detective to a fabulously rich jewellery designer.'

'A fabulously rich *exclusive* jewellery designer,' Lydia corrected with a wry grin. 'Here in Melbourne to sell my wares!'

'Well, whatever you are and wherever you're from, Graham's going to be kicking himself when he sees what a stunner you are underneath it all!'

'Underneath what?' Lydia frowned, but Maria wasn't going to elaborate.

Glancing at her watch, she grimaced. 'I'd better get over to the salon—and you'd better get ready to head to the airport. Santini's plane is just about due in.'

Lydia shook her head. 'I don't have to head to the airport—Graham and John are going to pull him out at Customs, to warn him about the security situation and escort him back to the hotel.'

'So when do you get to meet him?'

'In the restaurant. They want the initial contact to look completely accidental—I'm accidentally going to spill my drink on him. You'd think they could have come up with a better pick-up move than that! I'm supposed to be about to check out of the hotel, and he's apparently going to be so bowled over by me that he moves me straight up to his suite…' She could see Maria's lips twitching as she tried not to smile. 'That's the sort of thing he does, apparently. I'm going to look a right fool.'

'A gorgeous fool, though. I can't wait to see what you look like.' Maria rubbed her hands in delighted glee.

'Right, I'm going to have a quick shower, and then off to the parlour—are you coming?'

Lydia shook her head. 'You go ahead. I think I'll have a swim first, and try to wind down a bit.'

'Will you be okay?' asked Maria.

'I'll be fine.' Lydia smiled, and the smile stayed in place until Maria had closed the sauna door behind her.

Finally alone, Lydia allowed herself an indulgent moment. Raking her fingers through her damp hair, she rested her head in her hands, bracing herself for the huge task that lay ahead over the next few days—guarding a VIP with a security threat *in situ*. She had to push aside her own problems—or lack of them, now that it was over with Graham.

God, it was hot!

Lydia stepped outside the sauna, visibly blanching at the sight of the cool plunge pool and opting instead for the hopefully warmer lap pool.

Popping into a cubicle she pulled on the rather boring navy bathers she used for her daily swim, knowing that if she was going to carry off the part of Anton Santini's latest girlfriend she'd better head over to the boutique and buy a decent bikini. Folding her clothes and placing them in her bag, she padded out to the pool area, glad to see that it was deserted again, and glad for a few moments of solitude before the rigours of the next few days began.

A wealthy financier, Anton Santini part-owned a vast string of international hotels. According to the detailed brief Lydia had been given, his hotel chain was considering adding this luxury Melbourne hotel to its impressive list of residences. More importantly, down the track he was considering building a vast, brand-new hotel complex in Darwin, which would not only mean more tourists, but would also provide many vital jobs for the locals in the Northern Territory.

Everyone wanted his whirlwind visit to Melbourne to go well—hence the panic that had ensued when a potential security threat towards Anton Santini had been revealed. There had been no time to reschedule the gathering—he was already on his plane and heading for Australia—so instead red panic buttons had been pushed and a massive security operation had been hastily put in place—with no expense spared! And though professionally Lydia relished the opportunity, she was cringing at the prospect of playing the part of Santini's girlfriend. She knew that no amount of buffing and coiffing was going to bring her up to his exacting standards—she could still hear the sniggers from her colleagues when she had been chosen—but, worse, she could almost see the scorn and incredulity that would surely be visible in Santini's eyes when they were finally introduced.

Swimming always calmed her, and a half-hour of concentrating on her breathing, focusing on nothing more than reaching the cool marble at the other side of the pool, was exactly what she needed now. Dipping her toe in the inviting-looking pool, Lydia found it pleasantly warm, the deep blue water seemingly calling her to dive in and forget for a moment the pressures of modern living. Diving in gracefully, she closed her eyes as she hit the water, and felt the tension that had held her together disperse as she slid beneath the surface, propelling her body along the floor of the pool, her breath bursting in her lungs as she held it in.

* * *

It was good to be alone. Punching his desired level, Anton glanced at his expensive heavy watch as the lift descended from the Presidential Suite to the lower ground floor and realised that had he caught his scheduled flight then his plane would only just be landing now. He was infinitely grateful to the unknown first-class passenger on the packed flight that had preceded his who had cancelled, allowing Anton the luxury of five hours' sleep in a hotel bed before he faced his horrendous schedule.

Sitting in the luxurious surrounds of the first-class lounge, sipping on a brandy as he'd waited to board the earlier plane, in a reflex action he'd reached for his mobile to call his PA and tell her about the change. But then, almost defiantly, he had clicked his phone off, filled with an urge to have a few hours in his life that were, for once, unaccountable.

Feeling as if he was playing hooky, Anton had boarded the plane and, in a move that was so unusual for him it bordered on the bizarre, he'd handed over his laptop to the flight attendant and refused the latest copies of overseas newspapers. Shaking his head at the endless delicacies that were offered as the plane hit altitude he'd chosen instead to pull on a pair of headphones and gaze unseeing at the international news, his eyes growing heavy as it morphed into a film...

As the lift doors slid open, Anton Santini, automatically polite, pressed the button to hold it open for a dark-haired woman wrapped in a white robe. Her flushed faced indicated that she had just come from the gym area where he was heading. She did a double take when she saw him, but Anton didn't give it a thought.

He was more than used to women giving him a second look. His six-foot-three frame and dark Latin looks merited that alone, and given that these days there was barely a newspaper or magazine published that didn't contain a photo of him, it wasn't just women who looked twice.

It certainly didn't cross his mind that the dark-haired woman might be an undercover detective who didn't expect him to be in the country just yet! And it never entered his head that Maria was battling with a surge of panic because an unsuspecting Lydia was swimming in the pool—where, judging from the towel draped around his shoulders, Anton was clearly heading!

With a brief nod he stepped out, following the signs for the hotel pool and gym, noting with a wry smile that despite the fact he was in Australia, literally on the other side of the world, he might just as well be in Rome, or London, or Paris, or wherever his hectic schedule took him. No matter how much the hotels fought to be different, to stamp their originality in the minds of affluent businessmen, each and every one was pretty much the same.

Still, at least he had the place to himself.

Even as he processed the thought Anton retrieved and corrected it. As he had turned the corner he hadn't acknowledged the massive marble pool—he was used to extravagant surroundings, and the marble floor and glittering blue water had barely merited a glance. All he *had* noticed was the still surface of the water, the thick scent of chlorine, the silence of an empty room. But now, in a beat, his eyes were drawn to the long dark shadow beneath the water, to a hand breaking the surface tension, followed by a slender, pale arm arching a perfect stroke. As he went to walk on, to deposit his towel and robe on the bench, something held him back. In another beat, after another moment's hesitation, his eyes were drawn to the figure in the water. Her pale length was effortlessly gliding the length of the pool, titian hair dragging behind her, eyes closed as she rhythmically swam towards the edge, then executed a perfect tumble-turn before disappearing beneath the surface again for an impressive length of time.

Anton found himself drawn to the willowy figure. There was something about the effortless way her body moved, a natural litheness that held his attention—something different about this woman. He took a moment to fathom what it was: she was actually enjoying herself! Unlike most early morning swimmers in a hotel pool, she didn't appear to be working on toning her thighs or extending her endurance. Instead she seemed to be taking a moment, an indulgent moment, oblivious to her surrounds, and inexplicably he didn't want to disturb her, didn't want to invade this woman's privacy, didn't want to break her delicate stride.

But it was a hotel pool, Anton reminded himself with a brisk shake of his head. It wasn't as if he'd climbed a fence and stood in voyeuristic silence as the lady of the house swam in her back garden. Almost defiantly he pulled off his robe. Unlike Lydia, he didn't test the water for warmth, didn't gingerly dip in his toe—ice could have been floating on the surface and Anton would have merely dived straight in—and as Lydia neared the far end of the pool he slid into the water.

* * *

She felt his presence.

She couldn't really explain how she knew the presence was male, but as she felt the wedge of water buffet her slightly Lydia knew quite simply that it was, and, snapping out of her almost hypnotic trance she shifted back to an alert, edgy state. The effortless strokes she had been executing were more cumbersome now. Her breath was no longer coming regularly, her strokes were no longer deep and rhythmic, and she grasped the marble beneath her fingers, turned around and held onto the edge to catch her breath a moment.

Her eyes gazed the length of the pool, idly focusing on the man coming towards her, and suddenly, despite the width, it was as if the pool had shrunk. Maybe she was too used to the routine of her usual gym—the lanes neatly divided by a row of yellow buoys, swimmers keeping strictly their lanes—but he was heading straight for her, every stroke drawing him closer, long, muscled arms stroking their way nearer. Inexplicably she didn't move, just held onto the edge as he came in too soon, too fast.

'*Scusi.*' Even though it was the shallow end the water was still deep, but he stood his ground, didn't need to clutch the edge as Lydia did, shaking his black hair, blinking his eyes and facing hers. 'I thought it was bigger…'

'Me too.' She gave a small shrug, understanding instantly what he meant—the regular length of a pool like this was twenty-five metres, but this one fell a couple short, and if you were used to swimming—as this man clearly was—used to pacing yourself, it was an easy mistake to make. 'You soon get used to it.'

'Sorry!' He said it again, only in English this time.
Lydia actually preferred the more spontaneous response
he had used earlier, but there were other things on her
mind now. Her shrewd amber eyes focussed, and there
was a nervous swallow in her throat as she realised
that, way before schedule, the man she would be spend-
ing the next few days with, the man she should be 'accidentally' meeting in a few short hours, was actually
here.

Her mind raced for an explanation and her helpless
eyes darted around. She was half expecting to see her
colleagues Graham and John appear at the doorway, or
for Anton Santini to formally introduce himself, explain
that there had been a mix-up in the schedule and that
this in fact, was their accidental meeting.

That would explain it, Lydia decided in a split second.
That would explain why he had swum so directly towards her—would explain why she had been so acutely
aware of his presence, why his eyes were boring into her
as if he knew her—he *knew* who she was!

But, far from introducing himself, he gave her a small
nod before pushing away from the edge and swimming
off, leaving her standing there clinging to the edge, her
heart racing, her breath coming in small shallow gasps.
Only it had little to do with the exercise and everything
to do with the man who shared the pool. Her skin stung
from the brief touch of him, and goose bumps appeared
on her arms as she recalled the feel of his strong legs
brushing against hers. Her mind raced to calm itself, to
turn off the energy he had released, to switch off the
adrenaline that was pumping through her veins right
now. She didn't know what to do, unsure now if Anton

actually did know who she was, if her lack of response when he had tried to approach her had confused him.

Taking a deep breath, even though her body was tired now, Lydia knew that she had to swim on, to give Anton another chance to talk with her, mindful that if Anton was here then anyone could be watching. Her eyes glanced up to the security cameras. Even though it was only the two of them in the pool this meeting had to look accidental; the biggest threat to Anton Santini's safety was the fact that no one yet knew who the enemy was—no one knew how sophisticated the plans that were intended to bring him down might be.

Swimming a couple more lengths should have been easy, but her effortless stride eluded her now, and Lydia tried to fathom why she couldn't resume the simple strokes. She decided that the work-out, the swim, and then the surge of energy when she had realised that Anton was in the pool had left her depleted. Her body was heavy and leaden as she dragged it through the water, and her mind was spinning like a stuck CD—whirring furiously for a moment before playing aloud the single track she didn't want to hear...

He'd aroused her.

It had nothing to do with the fact it was Anton Santini—the man she was engaged to protect for the next few days—in the water with her. Instead it had everything to do with the man who had dived in just a few moments ago—a man she had been attracted to even before she had realised his identity. It was that thought that panicked Lydia, made every supposedly natural movement a chore, made this *chance* meeting all the more difficult.

'You must swim a lot?'

He was waiting for her at the other end, as she had known he would be, and his voice was deep, husky and heavily accented when he spoke. Heart hammering in her mouth, Lydia nodded.

'Most days,' she breathed. 'Though I think I've done too much this morning. I was working out before, and then I had a sauna…'

Lifting her hand, she gestured to the gym behind them, but Anton's gaze didn't follow where she was pointing. Instead she felt his dark navy eyes drag the entire length of her slender arm, scorching her pale flesh from her fingertips to her creamy clavicle. He took in every facet of the subtle muscle definition, of the pale tea-coloured freckles, then slowly worked his way up her long slender neck, searing her with his eyes. The flicker of her pulse in her neck, his nervous swallow, every tiny movement was accentuated until finally he looked directly at her. But there was no relief, only recognition—a jolting recognition, not of familiarity but of attraction. It was a powerful, faint-making emotion, terrifying exhilarating, and Lydia felt her panic multiply. She struggled to retract what her eyes had just stated, to tell this man that this was strictly business—that she was only here because it was her job. She was supposed to be meeting him in the hotel lounge in two hours, as she pretended to check out of the packed hotel—was supposed to spill a glass of water over him. Their attraction was meant to be mutual—so much so that Anton Santini would overcome the problem of a full hotel, would fall so much in lust with this stranger that he would, within

a matter of a few hours, install her into his bedroom.
That was the plan.

At this very moment Anton Santini was supposed to
be being pulled over by customs officers, and John and
Graham would deliver those very instructions.

What had happened?

Lydia didn't have time to guess—didn't have time to
go through the hows and whys. She had to swing her
mind away from the delicious distraction of his eyes and
force herself to operate—not as a woman, but as a detective. If the plans had changed then so must her approach—there wasn't exactly a glass of water handy to
spill over him right now!

'I'm Lydia,' she managed, forcing a small smile to
lips that didn't seem to want to obey. 'You are…?'

He didn't answer, just gave her a small, slightly
superior smile, his full mouth twisting upwards slightly,
his dark eyes still shamelessly staring. Lydia knew that
he didn't want to play along, and considered introduc-
tions completely unnecessary when they both knew who
they were dealing with—but *anyone* could be watching,
Lydia reminded herself. They *had* to act as if they were
strangers meeting, had to keep appearances up at all
times. She would reiterate that fact to Anton later, when
they were alone.

Alone.

Her stomach tightened at the mere thought. A knot
of anticipation gripped deep within, a blush spread over
her chest as a thousand inappropriate thoughts played
in her mind. She understood now how it happened—
understood how so many powerful, beautiful women
had fallen for him so completely and utterly—how they

had ignored his appalling reputation and thrown caution to the wind. The sheer, raw sensuality of the man was devastating, his presence overwhelming, blocking out reason, dimming rationality with the power and force of a solar eclipse. And right now, even if it was all engineered, that energy was focussed entirely on *her*.

Lydia struggled to reflect it. She struggled to keep a level head as her body begged a more primitive response. Angrier with herself than at him, her voice was more demanding, her eyes holding his boldly, as she insisted that he introduced himself. 'You are…?'

'I am…' His smile bordered on the cruel now, like a predator eyeing his victim. His gaze was inescapable as the massive room suddenly closed in around them, as the steamy warm air seemed set to suffocate her, the atmosphere so throbbingly sensual Lydia could almost hear the hiss of the temperature rising as he moved in closer '…going to kiss you…'

She didn't know what to do. Her head was telling her to pull back, reminding her that this level of intimacy wasn't in her job description. But instead she stared up at this stunningly beautiful man, her eyes wide, her body rigid with a curious dizzy expectation as his face moved towards her, sheer unadulterated lust drenching her far more than the water.

The morning shadow on his chin was almost as navy as his heavy-lidded eyes, his cheekbones exquisitely sculptured in his haughty face. Truly, Lydia decided, he was the most beautiful man she had ever borne witness to—such strength, such arrogance, even, etched in every feature. Yet his eyes were gentle as they held hers, soothing her terror and multiplying it at the same time. She didn't want to move, didn't want to back away from the pleasure that was surely to follow. Even if it was orchestrated, even if it was just for show, a tiny voice was telling her to go with it—a tiny, dangerous voice she'd never heard before was telling her that she didn't want to miss the feel of this beautiful man close to her, that never again in her lifetime was she likely to be kissed, to be held, by someone as supremely divine as Anton Santini.

Her eyes closed in giddy expectation as painfully slowly he moved in... But in a curious move his lips didn't meet hers. Instead he dusted his cheek against hers, the warmth of his breath tickling her face, and even if the kiss that was surely about to ensue was only for the cameras, for the sake of the hidden audience that might be watching, before his lips even met hers Lydia knew it would be one she would remember for ever.

His chin was scratching, dragging slowly along her pale, alert flesh, so slow it was almost painful. Yet it had the desired effect. His decadent stealth banished her fear and skilfully replaced it with need—a need that was physical, a need that was palpable. Her lips twitched with desire, her body flaming in its treacherous response to his touch, and lingering misgivings were gone completely. His touch had her moving her lips to his, and so magnetic was his force that reason and doubt were erased, and it was Lydia moving things along, Lydia's mouth searching for his, and finally, deliciously, finding it.

She relished in the bruising weight of his mouth against hers, the cool of his tongue as it parted her willing lips, the soldering feel of his hand in the small of her back as he pulled her a fraction closer, fanning the flames of desire. Her insides literally melting, she felt her fingers let go of the edge, but the bottom of the pool was too deep for her to stand. He supported her easily, her body weightless in the water, his arms holding her as his mouth ravished her, warm, muscular thighs tipping her further into heady oblivion.

Her swollen nipples were straining against Lycra, and heat was flaring between her legs. The need that imbued her was still not satisfied, the taste of such pleasure making Lydia greedier now, hungry for more. And Anton reciprocated. The nudge of his erection against her taut stomach was faint-making as she pressed provocatively against it, fuelling a primitive desire Lydia had never, not even in her most intimate moments, fully experienced—a total and utter abandonment, a complete, delicious loss of control.

He made her bold, made her wanton, provocative, immersed her in passion.

Her mind was completely focussed now on her own desires, on the pulse flickering between her legs. Her clitoris was engorged, twitching with want, and only this man could satisfy it. Still he kissed her, ravished her, but his mouth was moving now, tracing her neck, kissing the hollows. He buried his face in her dripping hair, and her fingers dug into his shoulders, and in a movement that was as provocative as it was instinctive she raised her hips several decadent inches. His fingers pressed into the warm flesh of her taut buttocks and the deep, languorous, throaty kiss was abandoned as she glided her swollen, most intimate lips along the endless, solid length of his manhood.

His breath was hot on the shell of her ear as she nestled the heat of her centre on the tip of his. She wanted him to take her, to part the tiny inch of fabric that covered her most private place. Wanted him to fill her, to calm the frenzy of her body beneath the still surface of the water. Her stomach tightened in rhythmic contraction and her legs wrapped around him as he pressed his velvet steel harder against her. Heady, drunken, faint, Lydia rested her head on a damp shoulder, nibbling at the salty flesh of his skin, willing him to take her, sure that the strength of his erection alone could part the fabric that covered her. She could feel the pulse of her orgasm aligning, the heavy pit in her stomach an abyss that needed to be filled. And, from the short, rapid breaths in her ear, the tension in every muscle beneath her fingers, Lydia knew he was as close as dammit too.

His hand moved from her, pulling impatiently at his bathers, the motion causing his knuckles to dig into the flesh of her inner thigh. The pain only intensified the experience, abandonment drenching her as she imagined him spilling his salty kiss inside her, visualised the decadence of Anton Santini making love to her…

Anton Santini!

The two words were a brutal slap to her flushed cheeks—a stab of self-preservation mercifully holding her back at the eleventh hour. The world suddenly came into sharp, unwelcome focus and she pulled back, struggled to catch her breath—appalled at what had taken place. She quivered with unsated desire as her mind fought for control and she stared at his questioning eyes.

This was work. This was her livelihood. But it wasn't just that that had stopped her. It was the knowledge, the realisation, that a man as suave, as sophisticated, as merciless as Anton Santini could reduce her in a matter of minutes to this squirming ball of desire. If she lost her head she'd go under; he would crush her in the palm of his hand and barely even notice.

'Lydia?' he murmured, clearly confused by the change in her.

'I have to pack…' She shook her head as if to clear it. 'I've got an appointment at the hairdresser…'

And he should have understood, should have been versed by Detective John Miller about the plan. But he just stared back at her. Lydia thought she understood his confusion—John would have told him that he wasn't to be left alone!

Her mind raced for a solution and almost instantaneously found one. 'We could go up to my room,' she said, suddenly desperate to get away from the pool, to find out just what the hell was going on and—perhaps more importantly—face this man dressed!

But she stopped talking abruptly as she heard loud chattering in the corridor outside. Aware of the potential precariousness of the situation she moved quickly, putting herself between Anton and the doorway.

'What are you doing?' He sounded irritated, confused by the change in her, but there was no time for explanation as Maria and another woman appeared. Although Maria was still dressed in her white robe a towel was rolled up under her arm, and Lydia knew that she was now armed.

'*Signor Santini, che cosa fa qui?*'

A large, irate woman Lydia could only assume was Angelina gesticulated wildly as she addressed her boss.

'*Sto nuotando!*' came Anton's curt reply.

Lydia bobbed under the water and swam towards the edge, her hands gratefully reaching the silver of the rail, dragging herself up the steps. It was as if the marrow had seeped out of her bones, and her legs were weak as she pulled herself out of the water and located her robe.

'I ask him what he is doing here so soon,' Angelina's exasperated voice greeted Lydia as she made her way over. 'And he say swimming—I had no idea he was coming!'

'Well, he's here,' Maria said, with a distinctly dry edge to her voice, frowning as she watched Lydia who, her fingers shaking, pale and wrinkled from her time in the water, was knotting her belt. 'Is everything okay?'

'Everything's fine,' Lydia said, hardly trusting herself to speak, still brutally shaken from her first encounter with Anton.

'Go up and shower quickly,' Maria said in low, urgent tones. 'Then get over to the salon. I'll cover him till you're dressed and ready—we'll get him upstairs and brief him.'

'Brief him?' Lydia blinked at Maria. Surely she had misheard? Or perhaps Maria didn't know that Anton had already been versed in the situation? That *had* to be the case, Lydia begged mentally. Because otherwise…

Panic rose in her as she attempted to confront the other appalling possibility—that Anton Santini really hadn't been briefed—that he had no idea who she was—that he had merely been attracted to her, had approached her, just as his bio suggested he would, with the supreme confidence that she would respond.

And she had!

'Where are John and Graham?' Lydia asked, trying to keep her voice even as Anton climbed out of the pool, her eyes darting away as she tried and failed not to notice the superb body that only moments ago had been pressed against hers.

'On their way back from the airport,' Maria answered, and Lydia's last vestige of hope disappeared—Anton really had no idea who she was. 'I rang them and told them what was happening.'

Cheeks flaming, she avoided even looking at him. Somehow she picked up her gym bag, and somehow she made her way out to the lifts, her heart hammering in her chest, only remembering to breathe when she was finally alone.

He would have made love to her if she'd let him, and—Lydia gulped as horrible truth flooded in—she almost had. She had almost let a virtual stranger in, let down her cool façade in an appalling unguarded moment. Anton hadn't just seen a different side to her character today, it was as if a complete *alter ego* had emerged—a wanton, sensual woman that knew her needs.

Oh, there *had* been a blistering attraction—that much she understood, that much she could accept. She could almost console herself that they had chosen to mix business with pleasure, had been caught up in the thrill of the moment, safe in the knowledge that they were making themselves look convincing to anyone watching... But if Maria was right, if he hadn't even known that she was a detective, that they were *supposed* to be meeting, then she wasn't just out of her depth with Anton Santini she had already been pulled under!

What sort of man had the confidence, the supreme arrogance, to approach a stranger and kiss them so blatantly, so fully, to arouse them to the point of oblivion and know, just know, that she would reciprocate—know that with one touch he would win?

On autopilot she headed for her room, showered and dressed quickly. She closed her eyes, her mind tightened in disbelief, a stinging flood of shame coursing through her body as another question exploded in her mind.

What must Anton think of her?

CHAPTER TWO

THE PRESSURE of the hairdresser's fingertips on her scalp as she massaged conditioner deep into her hair didn't even provide a vague distraction—Lydia's mind was working overtime, trying to fathom how she was supposed to face Anton Santini now. How on earth could she manage detachment, professionalism, after what had transpired in the pool? Hell, right now she'd settle for being able to look him in the eye.

But she had to remain in control—not only did her career depend on it, but Anton's life was in her hands. And, given she was signed up as his protector, her life too could be on the line. This was no time to be acting like a gauche teenager—she had to somehow regain control of this appalling situation, had to wrestle back her dignity. But for the first time in her life she was completely at a loss to come up with a plan. How could she deny her part in what had taken place? How could she deny the blatant, overwhelming passion that had engulfed her? The sensual, debauched *alter ego* that had emerged the second he had touched her?

'So, you're booked for nails, full make-up and a blow-dry?' Karen, the therapist questioned her as a

warm towel was wrapped around Lydia's head and she
was guided to the make-up room.

'Please.' Lydia nodded, lowering herself into the chair
and trying to sound blasé, as if she did this type of thing
every day. 'Though I'm not sure if there will be time to
do my nails. I've got an appointment scheduled—'

'That's no problem,' Karen interrupted, clearly used
to dealing with busy clients. 'Cindy can do your nails
while I do your make up—let's have a look at you.'
Pulling off the towel, she ran her fingers through Lydia's
long red curls.

'Is it business or pleasure?' When Lydia blinked
back, Karen elaborated. 'Your appointment? I'm just
trying to get a feel for how you want to look.'

'It's business,' Lydia answered firmly. 'And I want to
look fabulous!'

'Oh, you will.' Karen winked, tipping the chair backwards and setting to work.

Lydia closed her eyes as a few stray hairs around her
eyebrows were deftly tidied and a thick layer of scented
cream gently rubbed into her face, chatting amicably to
Karen about jewellery and the one-off pieces she supposedly designed, practising the alias she would be
adopting over the next few days.

'How long are you staying at the hotel?'

'I have to check out this morning.' Lydia gave a regretful shrug. 'When I checked in I was hoping to stay
for four nights but apparently the hotel's been booked
up for weeks—some VIPs are arriving this morning.
The bellboy's bringing my luggage down now, and
while I'm having breakfast the concierges are ringing
around to find me alternative accommodation.'

'That'd be right,' the therapist muttered. 'Kick out the paying guests…' Her voice trailed off as she realised she'd probably overstepped the mark, but Lydia pushed on, more than happy to fish a little, giving a tiny swallow as she tried to sound like the rich little madam she was hoping to portray.

'Well, I'm far from happy with the situation,' Lydia bristled. 'And I sincerely hope that a concierge can find me somewhere suitable—somewhere with a decent salon at the very least. What sort of VIPs are they anyway?'

'The worst sort,' the therapist answered in a theatrical whisper. 'There's going to be a take-over of the hotel and some of the bigwigs from a massive European chain are coming. We're all supposed to be on our best behaviour—why don't we try grey?'

'Sorry?' Opening her eyes, Lydia blinked back at the woman.

'On your eyes. I know you said you prefer neutral, but a deep smoky grey will really bring out the amazing colour of your eyes—they're more gold than hazel—'

'I don't want anything too heavy,' Lydia broke in. 'I really prefer a more natural look.'

'Trust me,' Karen insisted, a long red nail hovering over an array of tiny pots, her eyes narrowing as she stared closely at Lydia's face. 'You're going to look stunning. One wave of my magic wand and I can create an entire new you.'

A 'new you' was exactly what was needed, Lydia thought ruefully, if she was ever going to face Anton. A tiny glimmer of a plan started to emerge. 'Can you do anything to tone down my complexion?'

'You're as white as paper,' Karen tutted.

'But I blush terribly.' Lydia gave a dismissive shrug. 'And, like I said, I've got an important meeting this morning—I don't want to give myself away when we discuss prices.'

'You need a green base.' Karen nodded knowingly. 'Nothing like what you're thinking.' She grinned at Lydia's rather startled expression. 'I've got this fabulous mineral powder; we have it flown in from New York. Wearing that you can double your prices—triple them, even—and you'll be as pale and as cool as porcelain.'

'Really?' Lydia gave a dubious frown.

'Really!' Karen winked. 'We'll have to pay extra attention to your *décolletage*—that's a real give away when you're blushing.'

And she *would* blush!

Just the thought of facing Anton had her pulse pounding in her temples and a scorching, shameful warmth flooding her. But as Karen worked on slowly the horror receded, and Lydia gave in to the pleasure of the moment, knowing that in a few short days she'd be back to a few dabs of sunblock and slick of mascara if she was lucky.

Lydia let Karen transform her as Cindy worked on her nails. She didn't even glance in the mirror when she sat upright for her hair to be dried—she focussed on a magazine as her curls were dragged beyond her shoulders.

For the first time in ages Lydia didn't turn automatically to the health section, didn't read how she could increase her stamina or detox her entire system in a mere weekend. She even bypassed an in-depth article on a recent high-profile court case. Instead, with a flutter of excitement, she flicked to the social pages. She gazed at photos of the rich and famous, at their smooth botoxed faces belying their age, their divine dresses and long, smooth legs that ended in jewel-encrusted shoes. She could almost smell the expensive perfume wafting from their silicone-enhanced bosoms. She looked at the Russian-red lips smiling for the cameras, and for the first time since she'd checked in Lydia smiled back.

The diversity of her career hit home: only this time last week she had been on a stake-out, dressed in a navy tracksuit, a world away from the glamour she was *forced* to sample now, boxed up in a supposedly abandoned van for forty-eight hours. She had watched pimps and drug dealers infesting the vulnerable with their wares, staring through the bolt holes fitted with telescopes as weary prostitutes willed the morning to come, drinking endless cups of coffee to stay awake as she made small talk and tried to cheer up Kevin Bates—an inspector on the force she regularly worked alongside, a man she both liked and admired.

Forty-eight hours confined in his company, listening to him fret about his eldest child who was having his tonsils out that week, was a world away from what she was experiencing now! A freshly squeezed orange and guava juice was the order of the day, instead of her usual flask of coffee. Now, massive marble bathrooms replaced the rudimentary portaloo in the corner of the van that she'd had to endure so they didn't blow their cover by stepping outside.

It wasn't just a world away, Lydia corrected herself, but an entire universe from where she was now. And for a slice of time this opulent world was the one in which she was supposed to belong, with which she had been ordered to blend in. Lydia made a vow to revel in it the same way Maria was—to live the fantasy of being obscenely rich. She'd taken the bad over and over again. For the next few days she'd enjoy the good.

'You're done!' Karen's voice was triumphant as she pulled off the towel and gown and smoothed Lydia's hair over her shoulders. 'I'll get a mirror so you can see the back and sides.'

Normally for Lydia the mirror bit of a salon visit was an uncomfortable, painful experience—a mumbled *thanks* as she wondered how on earth she could correct the appalling creation, grappling in her purse to give a very undeserved tip as she blinked away tears. This time, however, she was trying hard to keep herself from smiling, desperately trying to remember that she was supposed to be used to this, that she was always *supposed* to look groomed and divine.

Staring at her profile from every angle, Lydia barely recognised herself. Her curls were a distant memory. Instead her hair shimmered in a straight silk curtain. But it wasn't just her hair that had her mesmerised—it was the entire package! The sparkling gold of her eyes as they peered out from underneath smoky grey lids was deliciously framed by her newly darkened lashes, and even her skin seemed to glow with healthy delight, a cheeky dot of colour on the apple of each cheek drawing her gaze to the dark, sexy red of her lips.

'Try it now.' Karen giggled.

'Try what?' Lydia asked, still mesmerised by her reflection.

'Think of your deepest, darkest secret, something that will make your toes curl with shame, and watch that make-up do its magic.'

So she did…

She relived in her mind the sheer abandonment that had doused her this morning. The stinging sensation of Anton's kiss, the cool of his mouth, the nibble of his teeth against the wedge of her tongue. She could almost feel the steel of his erection nudging her most private place. She could almost feel herself willingly overstepping boundaries that until today had always been firmly entrenched. Staring at her reflection, Lydia envisaged what had just a short while ago seemed impossible— facing Anton Santini, confronting the man she had revealed so much of herself to, staring deep into those cruel, sensuous eyes and somehow appearing in control, portraying the cool, detached detective that she was supposed to be, somehow pretending that he hadn't touched her so.

'Cool as a cucumber,' Karen enthused, and Lydia blinked back at her reflection, amazed that the therapist was right—her face was pale, not a hint of a blush darkened her cheeks. Her shoulders were creamy white against the flame of her dress and Lydia was infused with possibility…

Maybe she could pull it off.

Stare at Anton and tell him that he didn't move her.

Tell him that the scorching intimacy they had shared hadn't been pleasure but merely a duty—a cross she'd had to bear.

She would get through this!

And because she was supposedly rich, a mere detail like payment shouldn't even enter her head—with a swish of her fragranced hair Lydia should stalk out. But, rummaging in her bag, she peeled off a note and pressed it into Karen's hand. She shared a tiny smile as the woman's fingers gleefully closed around the crumpled paper before heading out into the massive foyer, staring at her luggage being wheeled through the foyer by the bellboy. A concierge was juggling a telephone call and two rather irate Americans and attempting to catch her eye—no doubt wanting to inform her of the reservation he'd made on her behalf. But Lydia deliberately ignored him, heading over to the restaurant instead, ready to face Anton again. But on her terms this time—not as the woman he had witnessed earlier, but as the detective she was.

CHAPTER THREE

'SHE OVERREACTS!' Anton's words were like pistol shots shooting across the Presidential Suite. Showered and dressed now, he wanted to get on with his day, wanted to end this ridiculous conversation and get on with his work. 'Angelina had no business calling the police without consulting me.'

'She tried to contact you, sir, but your telephone was turned off.'

Kevin Bates faced Anton and tried to bring the situation under control—Maria's attempts to explain things had been greeted with scorn, but it was hoped the more authoritative air of an inspector might calm things down. 'Sir, you don't seem to understand the seriousness of the situation. As Maria has tried to explain to you, we have serious concerns about your safety... We have reason to believe that there is going to be an attempt on your life—'

'Because of some flowers?' Anton snapped.

'Because of this.' Kevin handed him a neat typewritten card.

'It says "Welcome, Mr Santini." What has that to do with anything?'

'You have an excellent PA, Mr Santini. In fact, the reason we've been able to rule her out as a suspect is because it's her attention to detail that has enabled us to recognise the threat. The hotel usually provides a display of native Australian flowers for the Presidential Suite…'

'So?'

'These flowers were delivered to the hotel last night. They were ordered from a florist down the road and paid for in cash. The card was already typed up.'

'By who?'

'The florist can't remember—after all it wasn't a particularly unusual request. What is unusual, Mr Santini, is that an identical card and lilies were delivered to the hotel you were staying at in Spain six months ago, when you were shot at.'

'I was *not* shot at,' Anton countered. 'The police decided at the time it was a gangland fight I was caught up in. I was merely in the wrong place at the wrong time. It was just bad luck.'

'At the time, it appeared so.' Kevin nodded. 'However, Angelina gave a very detailed statement to the Spanish police—at the time of the shooting she was in her room, attending to correspondence. She should have been with you. Flowers had been delivered and she couldn't work out who they had come from—a seemingly insignificant detail, so insignificant that when flowers were delivered to your hotel room in New York still it didn't seem relevant…'

'I was nearly run over in New York…' Realisation was starting to hit, and his hand raked through his hair as he recalled the details. 'A car came straight at me, accelerating as it did so. I jumped just in time. My shoulder was dislocated but I knew I'd been lucky—the police said…'

'Wrong place, wrong time?' Kevin offered, and Anton nodded.

'These flowers are a calling card, Mr Santini. A warning that we have to take seriously. You've also been getting some nuisance calls, I believe?'

'A few.' Anton shrugged, but Kevin shook his head.

'Not according to your PA. During the last twelve months or so you've received numerous calls—so many, in fact, that not only the telephone company but the police in Rome are investigating. Am I right that in recent weeks they've become more frequent?'

Finally Anton conceded with a brief nod of his head. 'Who?' he asked. 'Who wants to harm me?'

'That we don't know,' Kevin admitted. 'Believe me, we intend to find out. However, our primary concern is your protection while you're here in Australia. Now, you're not to discuss this security operation—not even with your own staff.'

'Why not?'

'Because right now they're all suspects in this investigation.' As Anton opened his mouth to argue, Kevin overrode him. 'It's a possibility that we have to consider—for that reason your PA is the only one who is to know about the undercover operation in place. Maria will stay with Angelina, given that she has direct access to you, and we'll have other detectives in place in the hotel. Naturally we'll have a detective with you at all times. '

'How do you expect me to explain to my staff why a police officer is by my side? With all due respect, you do *look* like a police officer,' Anton said, impatience evident in his every gesture as his heavily accented voice filled the room.

'We're not that stupid, Mr Santini.' Kevin gave a wry smile. 'I can assure you that the detective shadowing you is going to blend in.'

'How?' Anton asked, more intrigued than annoyed now. 'I can see that we could pass off Maria's presence by explaining that Angelina needed some assistance, but…'

'Do you remember the woman in the pool this morning?' Maria asked, watching as Anton frowned. 'She was there when Angelina and I arrived.' When Anton's frown deepened Maria assumed it was because he was trying to place her. 'She had red hair, was doing some laps. You probably didn't notice her, but she's actually been in the hotel since yesterday, posing as a jewellery designer from Sydney here in Melbourne to showcase her work…'

'She's a *detective*?' Anton's voice was a hoarse whisper as realisation hit. Closing his eyes for a second, he replayed the morning's events. With the benefit of hindsight, his mouth tightened in rage. 'You are telling me that that woman is in fact a police officer?'

'No, Mr Santini,' Kevin answered patiently. 'For the next couple of days, according to everyone she meets, Lydia is a jewellery designer visiting Melbourne and is here to target some new clients. However, given that the hotel is full, she's checking out this morning. The bellboy is bringing her luggage down as we speak.'

'I thought you said that she was staying with me?'

'She is.' Kevin nodded, enjoying seeing this supremely powerful man momentarily flailing as he explained the carefully laid plans. 'Initially she was going to hang around the hotel until lunchtime but, given that you've arrived early, we've had to move things forward. You're going to chat her up, and after a brief exchange you'll invite her to stay with you. From our homework, sir, I don't think any of your staff will be remotely surprised to find you with a young lady *in situ* by the time they get here. By all accounts you're a pretty fast operator.'

Anton pressed his lips together, fighting back a smart retort because, though it galled him to admit it, Detective Bates was speaking the truth—no one would turn a hair if they arrived to find a beautiful woman on his arms. After all, it had happened on numerous occasions before.

'Once you're alone, Lydia will give you more details and try and glean any information from you that might give us some insight as to who this person might be. She'll also brief you about how the next few days are to be handled. But that conversation can only take place in your hotel room, and even then only when Lydia is satisfied that the room is secure and that you're definitely alone. Whenever you are out of your room or there is another person present you are to act as if you're lovers...'

Kevin paused for a moment, giving Anton time to digest the instructions. He was slightly bewildered by the stunned expression on Santini's face—the fact that his life might be in danger hadn't initially evoked even a hint of reaction, but now, Kevin decided, clearly shock was setting in and the truth must be starting to hit him. The Detective's voice was a touch gentler as he continued. 'Now, to make your initial contact look accidental, we thought you could make your way over to the breakfast bar—'

'What do you mean—*initial contact*?' Anton sneered,

desperately trying to regain some semblance of control, forcing himself to drag his mind away from Lydia and back to the conversation. What on earth was he talking about? Did this buffoon not realise it had already been made? That the *initial contact* had been well and truly taken care of?

But just as he was about to correct him, he checked himself. Long ago Anton had learnt that any knowledge, however unimportant it might seem at the time, was a vital tool that could be used later. That to keep the upper hand one had to be constantly ahead of the game. So instead he changed tack.

The sneer still in place, he voiced a different question. 'Why on earth would I go over to the breakfast bar? I do not serve myself. Did you think of that when you were making your plans?'

He didn't get an answer. The room fell quiet as Kevin's mobile phone trilled. 'She's ready.' Kevin nodded, quickly ending the call and nodding to Maria. 'Okay, Mr Santini, there are two detectives coming up in the lift. Their names are Graham and John. Don't talk to them—just treat them as you would any strangers— they're going to take the lift down with you and watch until you're in the restaurant. Once you're there, Lydia will walk in. Perhaps you could—'

'I do not need to be told by *you* how to chat up a woman,' Anton sneered, appalled now by what had taken place this morning, and more than ready to face this undercover detective and give her a piece of his mind. 'Come.' He snapped his fingers impatiently. 'Let's get this over with. Let's make this *initial contact*!'

CHAPTER FOUR

ORDERING his breakfast Anton glanced around the room, bracing himself for her entrance. To anyone watching he would look supremely in control as he flicked open the paper and read through the business section, but inside he was seething.

She had *used* him, had been playing a mere game with him; she was the one who had been in control this morning, and it stung like hell to admit it. A bitter taste of his own medicine had been served, and it was almost choking him to swallow it down.

What the hell had he been thinking anyway? Anton demanded of himself—aside from the fact she was a detective, what the hell had he been doing, practically making love to a stranger in a pool with no thought to birth control, no thought to the consequences?

She could have been anyone!

Anton's jaw tightened.

She was a damned detective!

He looked up from his paper and his racing mind stilled as a pale woman walked into the restaurant. His anger momentarily faded as he watched her cross the room. Maybe the bright early-morning Australian sun that streamed through the windows had dipped behind a cloud for a moment, shadowing the bright skylights of the restaurant because all of a sudden the vast sun-drenched restaurant seemed to dim. Even the noise seemed to fade—the clatter of knives and forks against plates, the rustle of newspapers, the chatter of his fellow diners, all blurring in the distance as Lydia became the sole power source.

Lydia, filling each and every one of his senses, her presence so electric, so consuming, it was as if he could taste again the cool decadence of her kiss, inhale again the sweet pungent fragrance of her arousal. Her presence was so potent that as Lydia crossed the room it was as if everything bar her had been plunged into darkness, as if they had been catapulted back to the weightless inti-macy of the pool. Anton felt hollowed out with lust as he watched the long, slender legs that had been wrapped around him just a short while ago cross the room. His body responded like some testosterone laden adoles-cent's, as he took in every last detail. The naked flesh that had seared his was encased now in sheer silk stock-ings; the feet that had been bare, the soles that had dusted his skin, were delicate in high strappy sandals; the feather-light toned body he had pressed his own against was draped in a burnt orange dress—a brave move, with her colouring, yet it clashed divinely. Exquisitely tai-lored, it skimmed the length of her torso, the superb, subtle cut of the fabric divinely accentuating the enticing swell of her breasts, and the jut of her nipples caused Anton's fists to clench as he quelled the tirade of desire that swept through him. The inappropriateness of his arousal was thankfully hidden under the table, but still he fought to douse it, willing himself to move, to reach for a drink, to do something to break the spell. But he simply couldn't drag his eyes away. The flame of hair cascading down her shoulders captivated him like a roaring fire—until sensibility took over.

This was the woman who had used him.

Even though her back was to Anton's table, Lydia could feel the searing heat of his eyes on her as he crossed the room. Horribly exposed, she felt like a helpless creature being quietly stalked, and though her senses screamed danger, although every fibre in her being warned her of his approach, because her colleagues were sitting at a table just a few feet away, because this was her job, somehow she feigned nonchalance.

Concentrating on keeping the tongs in her hand steady, she spooned strawberries onto her plate and carefully selected some canteloupe and Kiwi fruit. Her heart was in her mouth, every nerve was screaming, warning of his approach. Her fight or flight response kicked in, willing her to run, to flee this dangerous predator. But she stood her ground, her confidence inwardly wavering but determined to thwart the emotional attack Anton would surely deliver and deal with him professionally.

'We meet again.'

His voice was a low, silken drawl. The scent of him reached her even before his words did, making the hairs on her neck static in their response to him, yet she refused to turn, refused to jump, refused to let him glimpse how much he moved her. Instead she carefully piled two more strawberries onto her plate before finally offering her response.

'We do.'

'This is a pleasant surprise!' He was impossibly close now. She could feel the heat from his body, the suffocating, intoxicating power of his presence as he moved deeper into her personal space, and Lydia knew it had to be *now*—that if she were to have any chance of fulfilling her assignment, any hope of controlling any dangerous situation they might confront, then she had to assume control, had to wrestle her self-respect, her authority, back from this consuming man.

'Hardly a surprise.' A tiny nervous swallow went unnoticed with her back still towards him. She dragged in air, forced her face into a smile and, tossing her long red mane, she faced him. She registered with a surge of triumph the flicker of confusion in his eyes at her confident response and yet this newly found confidence almost instantly dissolved as the beauty she had witnessed earlier seemed multiplied now. His thick jet hair was still damp, and the heavy, opulent scent of his cologne filled her nostrils. The near naked body that she had been pressed against was dressed now, but even a sharp, exquisitely tailored charcoal-grey suit did nothing to detract from the body beneath. If anything his clothes accentuated his perfection—the heavy white cotton shirt a contrast against his olive skin, the luxurious gold tie expertly knotted around his neck the only splash of colour apart from his eyes—dark, liquid navy, a perfect deep blue. The colour was as dense as a bottle of ink—no silver flecks, no flashes of green, just a velvet blue that caressed her.

The sharp, sculptured planes of his bone structure, from the straight Roman nose to the almost Native

Indian slant of his cheekbones and the jaw that had
bruised the tender flesh of her face, was smooth now,
with just a smudgy shadow beneath the skin—a subtle,
powerful hint of what lay beneath…the beauty of this
man in the morning.

In a flash of self preservation Lydia flicked her eyes
away, forced herself to look downwards. But there was
no solace there from the brutal masculinity of him, and
her eyes worked the length of his body, from the wide
shoulders and broad chest to the flat, lean planes of his
stomach, the long, muscular legs encased in superbly
cut trousers. She was the predator now, flecks of gold
sparkling in her amber eyes and her voice even when
she spoke, the nerves that had threatened to drown her
abating now as with relish she delivered a question.
'Did you enjoy your swim?'

For a beat he didn't answer. Two vertical lines formed
between his eyes—her detached stance was clearly not
what Anton Santini was used to. 'I did.' He gave a curt
nod, his voice deep and confident. The telltale frown
between his eyes was gone now, but Lydia knew she had
confused him, knew he had been expecting a different
reaction entirely. 'Aren't you supposed to throw a glass
of water over me?'

A smile parted her lips a fraction, her eyebrows darting up at his questionable humour. If she'd had any
more money in her purse she'd have cheerfully handed
it all over to Karen. Whether or not the make-up had
worked she still wasn't sure, but the confidence an impossibly expensive jar of make-up gave was proving in-
valuable—coupled with the assurance in her mind that
her hastily formed plan would work.

'That was before…' Lydia said in a low voice, enjoying the confidence of her *alter ego*, enjoying playing the part of a beautiful spoilt woman used to dealing with rich men.

'Before what?'

'Before,' Lydia repeated, watching his harsh expression soften momentarily and feeling her own aloof façade recede a touch as the intimacies they had shared just a short while ago reared in their minds. 'We can't talk about it here.'

'Where can we talk about it?'

He was back in control now, taking the loaded plate from her with one hand and guiding her towards his table with the other. She was infinitely grateful that he'd taken the small breakfast plate. Even that tiny task would have been too much for her now. She could feel the heat from the palm of his hand in the small of her back as he led her across the room like a puppet on a string, dancing to his tune again. As he pulled back a chair for her, as a waiter appeared and spread a thick napkin across her lap, Lydia glanced across and saw Graham and John just a few feet away, seemingly engrossed in their newspapers. But she knew they were watching, knew that their eyes were on her and Anton and the seemingly initial contact they were making, and it gave her the impetus to centre, to focus on the task in hand instead of the man opposite…to face her burning shame with clear, unwavering eyes.

Nodding a vague thanks as the waiter filled up her coffee cup and melted into the background, Lydia waited till they were alone before answering his loaded question.

'Before the plans changed,' she responded. 'Before

I realised that you'd come on an earlier flight and contact had to be made sooner.'

'Contact!' His word cracked the air like a whip, but Lydia deliberately didn't flinch.

'Convincing contact,' she elaborated with a hint of wry smile. 'I was merely following procedure.'

'Procedure?' Jet eyebrows shot into his hairline, his accent thick, every word loaded with menace. 'Is making love to your subject part of your job? Is this what you expect me to believe? I was told you were a police officer, not some *prostituta.*'

As vile as his words were, Lydia swallowed them. His version was far safer than the truth. If Anton even glimpsed the effect he had on her then both their lives could be in danger.

Selecting the plumpest, ripest strawberry, Lydia drizzled a spoonful of sugar over it, watching as the white crystals dissolved, refusing to jump to his impatient command. Taking her time to ensure her answer to his accusation was the right one.

'I was following your procedure...' Gold eyes glittered as she confronted him. 'To make it look convincing I was following yours—see a girl and pick her up...' Lydia's voice had a taunting ring. 'I'm not the easy one here, Anton—it's you.'

'No.' Angrily, proudly, he shook his head. 'You try to tell me that it was a set-up? That you engineered what happened, because of some threat—'

'We'll talk about this later,' Lydia broke in. His anger, his impending indiscretion were so clearly visible that even Graham was folding his paper, glancing over with a questioning look as Lydia quickly brought the situation under control. 'I refuse to discuss it here, Anton.'

And something in her eyes halted him, told him that she was serious. His tirade, but not the question in his eyes, abated as a concierge appeared, wringing his hands in abject apology as he clearly recognised Lydia's breakfast companion.

'Miss Holmes, I have made a provisional booking for you in a nearby hotel. It's just a few streets away…'

'Why can't she stay here?' Anton's question was curt, authoritative, and had the poor concierge stammering as he tried to answer. 'Are you telling me there isn't a single vacant room in the place?'

'There is,' the concierge attempted. 'But only standard rooms are vacant. All of the luxury suites are booked, sir. I explained this personally to Miss Holmes when she checked in—I told her that the suite she is occupying now was only available for one night, and that after that it would have to be a standard room—which naturally isn't suitable for her needs.'

'Then find her a room that is!' Anton's voice had an ominous ring to it, and for a moment Lydia forgot that he was acting, her top teeth nervously chewing her bottom lip as he voiced his demands. He was clearly used to getting his own way, clearly expecting his demands to be met, and from the tension in the concierge's face, from the nod of his head, they were about to be. Lydia realised with a start that despite Anton's convincing protests, separate rooms were actually the *last* thing either of them wanted.

'I will see what I can arrange…' Nervously, he addressed Lydia. 'Miss Holmes, would you have any objection to staying in one of our mini-suites? They aren't as luxurious as the suite you are in now, but I could ask the staff to—'

'No,' Lydia broke in, and the concierge's hastily arranged solution thankfully disintegrated. Clearly Inspector Bates hadn't fully factored in Anton's enviable pull when he had dreamt up this particular scenario, and she swallowed her guilt as she fixed the concierge with her most withering superior stare. 'I'm not interested in being *downgraded!* Could you please arrange a car?'

Standing, she smoothed her dress, picked up her shoulder bag and started to walk towards the foyer, deliberately avoiding her colleagues' panicked looks, praying inside that Anton would take his cue and rescue the situation.

'Move Miss Holmes's belongings to my suite.' His deep, commanding voice stilled her, and, turning, she watched Anton stare unblinking at the concierge.

'To *your* suite, sir?' The concierge checked, his eyes swivelling from Anton to Lydia.

'That's what I said,' Anton responded.

'You want luggage in taxi?' The bellboy's Italian accent had none of the liquid notes of Anton's, and his attempt at English was crude as he loudly approached the table, causing a couple of diners to look up. Lydia bit down on her lip in mortification as the concierge corrected him.

'No, there's been a change of plan. Miss Holmes will be staying with us after all. Could you take her luggage to suite 311?' The concierge's behaviour was impeccable as he addressed the bellboy. Not by a flicker did he betray what he was surely thinking.

'Suite 311?' The dark features of the bellboy screwed into a frown. 'But that's Mr Santini's suite—'

'Take the bags now, please,' The concierge broke in, clearly irritated that the bellboy had voiced the obvious to anyone within earshot.

As realisation dawned on the junior staff member, the contempt in his black eyes was visible as his gaze met Lydia's. The background chatter on the nearby tables stilled for an impossibly long time as in one crushing moment she changed from executive to escort, and not even the latest make-up direct from New York could fade the blush that spread over her face, over her entire body. Even her hands seemed to burn as she clenched them by her sides and willed this uncomfortable moment to be over.

'Now, come here.'

The derisive tone to his voice as Anton addressed her was like a slap to her cheek. With a flick of his hand, he summoned her to his table, gestured for her to sit down, and even if it was part of the plan, even if he had done the right thing, even if it was her job, Lydia felt a sting of humiliation as she walked back towards him. A burning anger within her flamed at his arrogance, his presumption, and she fought the desire to turn tail and run, or to lift her hand and slap that mocking cheek as she witnessed the glint of triumph in his eyes at her apparent submission. She saw his lips twist into a cruel smile as she obeyed his command and sat down at his table and she was imbued with shame, acknowledging how it surely must appear to all who were watching.

'Take Miss Holmes's bags up to the Presidential Suite.' Anton's voice broke the heavy silence. He stared directly at Lydia as he spoke, and even though the flames of anger and shame licked the sides of her throat, still his voice caressed her, still he managed to fan her desire. Hollowed with unwelcome lust, her heart seemed to stop beating as Anton spoke on, caressing her with each dangerous word, terrifying her with each skilfully seductive syllable. 'She is to be my guest—my very special guest—and I expect her to be treated as such.'

CHAPTER FIVE

'WILL THAT be everything, sir?'

Lydia paced uncomfortably as the last of her bags was deposited into the room by the bellboy. Clearly Anton had a lot of questions to ask, and after his arrogant performance Lydia certainly hadn't been in the mood for chit-chat over breakfast. The sooner Anton Santini heard the ground rules the happier she would be—and once the bellboy was gone, finally they would be alone.

'Not quite,' Anton clipped. 'Can you tell my team that I'm not to be disturbed? I'll meet them as arranged—I've booked one of the boardrooms for twelve.'

'I will make sure they are aware of your wishes.' The bellboy gave a small nod, but still didn't make a move to leave, staring instead at Lydia. Again she was uncomfortable under his scrutiny, embarrassed at what he perceived her to be. 'Would you like the butler to come and unpack for you?'

'I would like to be left alone. Put the "do not disturb" sign on the door on your way out,' Anton retorted briskly. Then, when still he didn't move, Anton pulled out his wallet, pressing a fold of notes into the younger man's hands, whistling an impatient, *'Grazie,'* through gritted teeth.

'Thank you,' the bellboy responded, and Lydia found herself frowning at his response, given that both men were clearly Italian. 'Enjoy your stay.'

Even though there were plenty of things she wanted to say to Anton, even though angry words bobbed on her tongue, as the door closed behind them Lydia still couldn't say what was on her mind. The room had been thoroughly checked only a couple of hours before, but it was up to her to ensure it was still safe. After locking the door and putting the chain on Lydia made idle small talk as she did just that.

'Gorgeous room,' she said, her voice casual. 'The bathroom's divine.' Her words were utterly at odds with her actions as she unzipped her shoulder bag and pulled out a handgun, placing it in the bedside drawer before carefully checking the suite, opening each and every door, looking under the bed, behind the mirrors and pictures, even in the lush arrangements of fresh flowers. Anton frowned, clearly bemused by her actions.

'Is all this really necessary?' When Lydia didn't deign to respond, instead carrying on with her careful check of the room, Anton's palpable impatience upped a notch. 'I asked you a question.'

'I think we need to set some ground rules,' Lydia responded crisply. 'Firstly—I'm here for your protection, Anton, and believe it or not I do happen to know what I'm doing. So please don't question my every move.'

'Suppose these people come into the room at three a.m.?' Anton retorted. 'I hate to tell you your job, but what good is a gun in a bedside drawer with its owner asleep?'

'None at all,' Lydia answered. 'I won't be sleeping, Anton. I'll rest during your meetings.'

'So at night you stay awake?'

'That's right,' Lydia said crisply.

'At night you watch me sleep?' The question was delivered in the same direct manner, his eyes still holding hers, and not by a flicker did he change his expression, but somehow Anton managed to shift the tempo, somehow he managed to reignite the crackling sexual tension, and Lydia moved quickly to douse it.

'I won't be watching you, Anton; I'll be watching the door.'

'It will be a long night for you.'

'I'm used to it,' Lydia said, attempting to be dismissive. 'I don't mind at all.'

'Why not? Do you get paid overtime?'

Her pay packet was none of his damn business. But it wasn't so much the question that infuriated her as the almost imperceptible implication, and the anger that had suffused her downstairs when he'd summoned her to his table emerged again.

'That's none of my business.' Anton answered his own question, then moved swiftly on. 'Secondly? I assume there's more?'

'You are not to leave this room without informing me—either I will accompany you downstairs—'

'Am I allowed to go to the bathroom by myself?'

Ignoring his facetious comment, Lydia attempted to continue with the brief, but Anton wasn't listening. He'd turned his back to her, pulling a small silver laptop out of his case in a clearly insolent gesture.

'I haven't finished yet,' Lydia said. But instead of

turning around to face her, infuriatingly, he opened up his computer and turned it on. 'I'm talking to you, Anton.'

'Then talk.' Anton shrugged, ignoring the warning note in her voice. 'I do not have to see you to listen.'

This only enraged her more, and gave her the final impetus to say what was on her mind. 'Finally, let's get one thing very clear—I know you don't want me here, Anton, and I know you think I'm clearly not up to the job, but don't you ever treat me the way you just did downstairs.'

'I assume we're talking about the restaurant rather than the pool?' Anton asked, pulling up files on his screen, long dark fingers stroking the keys, absolutely refusing to turn around. 'Because from memory you seemed to be enjoying yourself…'

'I'm talking about in the restaurant,' Lydia snapped. 'Insinuating that I'm some sort of escort, trying to embarrass me…'

Lydia wasn't sure what she had expected from Anton—contrition, perhaps, or an attempt at an apology—but the anger that had been simmering inside her exploded out of control as he threw his head back and had the audacity to laugh.

'It isn't funny.'

'I am told that I have to chat you up. I am told by your seniors that I am to arrange for you to stay in my room after only the briefest of meetings.' Finally he faced her, the computer forgotten as he stood up and turned around. 'Tell me, Lydia, how the hell were you supposed to come out of that encounter looking anything other than a cheap tart? Did you expect to come out of it looking like a rescued nun?'

'Of course not,' Lydia retorted but Anton hadn't finished and he walked two dangerous steps towards her. There were several metres still between them but even the slightest forward motion of this man had her mentally ducking for cover, had the vast Presidential Suite shrinking to a broom cupboard as he held her with his eyes.

'You say that people are watching.' His voice was coarse and direct. 'You say that that I have to act normally, that these people will know if I act in a different way.'

'Yes,' Lydia croaked, her mouth impossibly dry, her eyes wide as still he came closer. She tried to stall him with words, tried to put her point across while there was still space between them. 'And maybe you're used to women who—'

'Oh, I'm used to women,' Anton broke in, still a couple of feet away, but suffocatingly close now. 'I *know* women,' he breathed. 'I know all the games they play…' His voice trailed off, a muscle flickering in his cheek as he stared down at her. 'And believe me, Lydia, I have never once needed to pay for the pleasure of a woman's company—and anyone watching, anyone who knows about me, knows that to be true.'

'So what was that about downstairs?' Lydia pushed. 'Summoning me to your table, ordering me to sit. If I hadn't been on duty, Anton, I'd have walked—'

'You'd have sat,' Anton cut in. 'And that isn't a compliment.'

'I don't take it as one,' Lydia retorted. 'You're so damn sure of yourself,' she choked, appalled at his arrogance. 'You're so sure that with one crook of your finger you can have any woman you want—well, you're wrong. I'm here because of work, Anton, and believe me, I'm not enjoying myself.'

'You were a couple of hours ago,' Anton pointed out. 'Don't try and tell me otherwise.'

'You're a great kisser.' Somehow she kept her voice even, somehow she stayed calm. 'Maybe practice does make perfect after all—but it was strictly work for me.'

'Liar.' Anton smiled slowly, playing his trump card, recalling Inspector Bates's words and carefully watching her reaction as he relayed them. 'I spoke with your boss. I know that you weren't expecting me in the pool—the same way I wasn't expecting you, Lydia. This morning wasn't about work. It was about attraction.'

'No.' Slowly but surely she shook her head, red hair shimmering as the morning sun captured it. 'I thought you had been briefed, that you were fully aware I was a police officer. I was told that our initial meeting had to look authentic. I was just glad that as luck would have it Anton Santini didn't turn out to be five foot two with a beer belly. I guess even in the dirtiest of jobs there are flashes of silver.'

'So that kiss we shared…' He didn't look so assured now, his voice trailing off, those dark eyes for the first time confused.

'Was for the cameras.' Lydia finished for him. 'At least it was on my part. Though I have to admit—' she gave a small laugh '—it was extremely pleasurable.'

'We nearly made love,' Anton pointed out. 'We nearly—'

'No, Anton, we didn't.' Every word was a lie, every word a supreme effort, but a necessary one. She knew with certainty that she had to take the heat out of this encounter—had to somehow erase all that happened. And this was the only way she knew how. 'I pulled back—remember? I might have to crawl into your bed for the next couple of mornings to make things look convincing when the maid comes in. I might have to hold your hand as we walk down the hotel corridor, or even kiss you in front of a crowd, but don't for a minute think that it's about you and I. This is what I do for a living. I'm an undercover cop, and immersing myself in a role is something I'm used to. You were the one who kissed me, Anton,' Lydia reminded him. 'You were the one who swam over to a virtual stranger for no other reason than sexual attraction. I, on the other hand, was working.'

'Prostituting yourself!' Anton sneered.

'Trying to save your life,' Lydia countered. 'Though I have to admit sometimes I wonder why I bother.'

'I didn't ask for your help,' Anton pointed out. 'In fact, if it were up to me I would prefer to take my chances alone rather than have a—' He didn't say it, stopped himself before it continued, but the word was as audible as if he'd shouted it.

Lydia shook her head as yet again he questioned her competence and she finished the sentence for him.

'Than have a *mere* woman protect you?'

'I didn't say that,' Anton refuted. 'But if you insist on the truth then, yes—I admit that is how I feel.'

And Lydia could only grudgingly admire his honesty as he elaborated, because finally here was someone who actually voiced what half the station she worked at secretly thought. Here was someone who had the guts to speak his chauvinistic mind.

'I cannot possibly see how a woman half my weight,

who does not even reach my shoulders, has any hope of protecting me…' Anton's hands were gesturing wildly as he spoke, relegating her substantial height to that of a five-year-old. 'Maybe you are an expert at martial arts—who knows? But a black belt won't stop a bullet. This is not suitable women's work.'

Even making allowances for a rather poor translation, Anton's take on things was brutally obvious. His utter disregard, his sheer lack of respect for her had been made crystal clear.

'What *is* suitable women's work, Anton?' Lydia asked, her face chalk beneath her rouge, lips rigid with rage. 'Barefoot and pregnant in your kitchen?'

'You are being ridiculous,' Anton hissed.

'No more ridiculous than the assumptions you have just made about me—but at least my assumptions are based on fact. I've read up on you these past few days, Mr Santini.'

'What? You've flicked through a few glossy magazines to form an opinion?' Anton sneered. 'That would be about your level.'

'You arrogant bastard,' Lydia whispered. ' Maybe the only role you feel suitable for women is on our backs, with our legs wrapped around you, massaging your already over-inflated ego, but other people's lives may be at stake here—not just yours. There are innocent guests at this hotel, children staying here, and not for a second will I or my team allow their safety to be compromised. So you'd better start playing the game, Anton. For the next couple of days, like it or not, you're stuck with me—and whatever problem you have dealing with that fact, I suggest you bury it.'

Turning she headed for the bathroom, closing the door behind her and resting her shaking hands on the cool black marble, staring into the mirror at the made-up face she barely recognised, swallowing bile as she recalled the vile words that had hissed between them. Somehow they had managed to derogate the pure, naked beauty that had shrouded them this morning, had taken away the raw pleasure of that intimate moment until all that was left was a filthy smear of shame.

Flicking on the cold tap, Lydia ran her wrists under the water, willing herself calm, collecting her thoughts before heading back into the sumptuous room. She was expecting a second onslaught. Expecting Anton's fury to have been exacerbated by her absence and for the on-slaught of questions to start again. But as she stepped into the lounge, her stilettos not making a sound on the thick woollen carpet, for a second Lydia felt as if she were intruding.

His back to her, Anton was gazing out of the massive windows, but there was a loneliness to him that hadn't been there before, a weariness she was sure she hadn't seen, and it unsettled her—a flash of fragility in this fiercely proud man, a tiny chink in his armour that she was sure he hadn't meant to reveal.

'Anton?' The brittle edge had gone from her voice, but she waited for his mask to slip back on, for his haughty indifference to emerge as she crossed the room, but still he stared out of the window, and his voice was low and soft when finally it came.

'I apologise.'

Not for a moment had she expected an apology. The best she had hoped for was a tense stand-off. But somehow Lydia knew his words were heartfelt, somehow she knew that a man like Anton wouldn't apologise unless he meant it.

'I go too far.'

'You do?' Lydia gave a tiny, tight smile, taken aback by the sudden change in him. 'I do too,' she admitted.

'This morning has been…' She watched as he struggled to find the appropriate words, his hands clenching in frustration, and Lydia said them for him.

'A shock?'

He gave a slow nod.

'More often than not these security alerts come to nothing,' Lydia explained, more gently now. 'Certain events trigger alarms and we have to explore every avenue. It doesn't necessarily mean that—'

'That isn't what is bothering me,' Anton said with a tiny flick of his head.

'Then what is?'

Slowly he turned, the pain in his eyes hitting her with such intensity she took a step backwards. But he recovered in an instant, his stance snapping back to normal, a brittle smile inching over his lips as he scathingly answered her question. The mask had slipped back on with practised ease, just as she had known it would.

'Anton—' Lydia's voice was wary '—do you have any idea who it is that might want to harm you?'

'No.'

'Do you have any enemies?' Lydia pushed, frowning when he shrugged dismissively.

'Too many to name—'

'Anton, if you have any idea who might be behind all this, then it's imperative that you tell me. If you think—'

'My thoughts are my own, Lydia,' Anton snapped. The mask was firmly back in place now—no glimpse of the pensive side to him she had just glimpsed. 'Not even *you* can access them. Now, if you can let your colleagues know, I'd like to head down to the boardroom and get on with my day.'

CHAPTER SIX

IT WAS a relief to leave him at his meeting—a relief to come back to the room, lock the door and finally let her own mask slip for a few hours. To undress and pull the curtains and slide into the massive bed that he would inhabit tonight, and force herself into a few hours of Anton-inspired restless sleep.

The vibration of the pager on her bedside table informed her that the meeting would soon be closing, told her to get dressed and make her way down to the bar. Eyeing her wardrobe, Lydia stared at her rather pale offerings. The faithful black dress that *always* fitted the bill seemed drab and lifeless now. Her wardrobe wasn't quite up to the sophisticated world Anton inhabited. She was unsure if she could get away with wearing the dress she had worn earlier—the one truly fabulous item in her wardrobe, which had been borrowed from her incredibly glamorous younger sister.

It would have to do.

Again!

Dressing quickly, and heading to the bathroom, Lydia rinsed her mouth and touched up her make-up and perfume. She carefully placed the gun in her specifically designed handbag—a holster was considered too much of a risk if it were seen—then took a moment to check her reflection in the vast full-length mirror. The controlled, elegant woman who stared back at her was the antithesis of how she was feeling—her emotions were as friable as an adolescent's—but her glittering eyes were the only indicator of the fizzing arousal he had so easily instigated.

Checking her bag was in position, feeling the heavy weight of the gun against her side, Lydia let her eyes linger on the massive opulent bed of the Presidential Suite. She tried not to picture his jet hair on the golden pillow… Tried not to visualise that haughty guarded face softened by sleep… Tried not to imagine herself lying beside him…tried and failed on all three counts.

As dangerous and unpredictable as the night might be, the real danger to her wasn't what lay ahead in the bar, or on the walk back to the suite. The real danger for Lydia would be right here in this room. She had to keep her guard up, had to remain eternally vigilant, had to watch out not just for his life, but for her heart.

There was no question of heading over to the bar and ordering her drink.

As Anton Santini's *special guest,* Lydia acted accordingly—taking a seat on one of the low, velvet lounges and barely looking up as an attentive waiter came and asked what she would like to drink.

'Strawberry daiquiri,' Lydia answered, glancing briefly over to the bar to ensure that Kevin had seen her arrival. It was important that no one suspected even for a second that she was carefully observing proceedings, and if she was being watched a glass of mineral water might raise suspicion. Kevin had been placed at the bar to work as a member of the staff. His seniority was needed to oversee things, and also to ensure that, as much as possible, all the undercover detectives' drinks remained alcohol-free.

As the VIPs started to drift in from their meeting, Lydia didn't even need to turn her head to know when Anton arrived. The noise of background chatter and laughter dropped a touch, conversation momentarily suspended as he entered. The staff snapped to attention and Lydia noted that even the most beautiful of women checked themselves. Their hands dashing to their faces, flicking their hair, pulling in already toned stomachs, tongues licking at beautifully rouged lips, eyes narrowing a touch as their gazes followed the focus of this beautiful man's attention. Because he filled the room as he stepped inside—brooding yet somehow charismatic, with an elusive quality that had everyone paying attention.

What Lydia had expected of Anton, she wasn't sure—perhaps for the same chauvinistic arrogance she had witnessed in the restaurant to emerge again, or a brief, distracted introduction to his colleagues and acquaintances. But his attention was solely on her, his eyes fixed on her and only her as he crossed the room, dismissing his entourage. Clearly whatever had needed to be said in the meeting had been dealt with, and Anton was now off duty.

And stunning, to boot!

As he crossed the room, his purposeful stride heading directly towards Lydia, his restless eyes focussed solely on her, it was all too easy for a tiny dangerous moment for Lydia to indulge herself, to pretend that this was her reality—that the elegant, intimate smile softening his mouth was truly for her.

'How was your meeting?' Lydia asked as he sat down beside her on the low couch. The forced closeness was more intoxicating than any liquor, his thigh pressing against hers, his voice low and deep. Because of the background noise, Lydia had to lean forward to catch it.

'That is not how you would greet me if you were my woman.' His warm hand slid behind the curtain of her hair, his fingers massaging the back of her neck. Tiny pulses of energy flicked through her body as his mouth moved towards hers. '*This* is how you would greet me.'

He tasted of danger.

His kiss was a dangerous, teasing elaboration of the fantasy she had just harboured. And, as sexist and chauvinistic as his words were, they caused a flutter of excitement in the pit of her stomach—to be *his* woman, to greet this divine man with the deepest of kisses, had Lydia literally trembling inside. His tongue slid around hers, and his utter lack of inhibition, the complete inappropriateness of his actions, caused a shrill of excitement in her groin.

'That's better!' Pulling back, he lifted the drink that had been placed before him, completely calm, seemingly unmoved.

Lydia's eyes darted to Maria's, and she tried vainly to ignore the shocked but gleeful expression on her colleague's face.

'Now, how about we head for the restaurant?'

'I'd rather eat in the room,' Lydia attempted, the detective in her anxious to get him away from the crowd and to the relative safety of his suite. But when Anton shook his head and headed for the restaurant Lydia had no choice but to follow, her lips tight as Kevin delivered an annoyed frown in their direction.

Naturally Anton made an entrance as he entered the restaurant, with every face turning to look at the dark, brooding gentleman as he was whisked away to a discreet corner table.

There was an uncomfortable moment as Lydia ignored the chair that was pulled out for her, choosing instead the one that was being held out for Anton—to enable her to face the room and watch out for any irregularities.

'Sorry, I forgot,' Anton said as she sat, and for a second she was privy to one of his most charming smiles. Not for the first time Lydia wondered how on earth she was going to get through this—because Anton wasn't the only one struggling to remember why she was here. His gaze was so captivating, his company so overwhelming, it took all her strength to remain focussed, to break away every now and then and work the room with her eyes instead of staring into his. Waiters were hovering, pouring water, spreading a huge napkin over Lydia's trembling knees as Anton dealt swiftly with the wine list.

'Red?'

'Just water, thank you.'

'Water?' Anton looked truly appalled, but Lydia was insistent, taking the massive menu and trying to quickly make her way through it—which, after such a thorough kissing, was a feat in itself. Somehow Lydia stumbled through it, choosing a simple risotto as Anton ordered a massive rare steak, making small talk as the waiters flurried around them, but once they were alone Lydia managed to say what was on her mind.

'Don't do that again, Anton. If I say we go to the room, then that's what we do.'

'You like your work?' Anton asked, completely ignoring her anger.

'I love jewellery,' Lydia responded tightly, her eyes working the room, but relaxing slightly when she saw John and Graham being guided to a nearby table.

'Have some wine,' Anton pushed. 'It's really very good.'

'I can't drink any alcohol,' Lydia answered, her eyes imploring him to understand. Anton just frowned back at her, but thankfully changed the subject.

'So, your boyfriend—what does he think of your job?'

Not so thankful perhaps!

Giving him a tight smile, Lydia reluctantly answered—realising they would arouse suspicion if they sat in silence, but not too sure how much of herself to reveal. 'My ex-boyfriend hated it.' Lydia gave a tight smile. 'Even though he was in the jewellery business too. I've had a bit more success than he has lately—I think he may have been jealous.'

'Or concerned?' Anton quipped, and Lydia gritted her teeth. 'I wouldn't like my woman in that kind of work.'

'Your woman?' Lydia gave a tight smile. 'Whatever you were trying to say, Anton, it didn't translate very well.'

'It translated perfectly,' Anton answered, not remotely fazed. 'It's not a very feminine job—though I have to say you look amazing tonight. That dress, however, is a touch familiar. Maybe tomorrow I take you shopping.'

If it had been a real date she'd have slapped his damned face. 'Maybe not!' Lydia snapped.

'You are…' He paused for a second as he chose his words. 'One of those feminist women, yes?'

Lydia's jaw dropped at his cheek. 'What I am and what I believe in has absolutely nothing to do with you—'

'But we are on a date!' Anton flashed a devilish grin. 'Surely we are supposed to be getting to know each other better, Lydia?'

He had a point—and, given that her colleagues were close, and that the background noise of the restaurant meant there was no chance of them being overheard, by the time their meals arrived Lydia had relented a touch, dropping her defensive guard a notch, but only so as to find out more about *him*.

'Do *you* enjoy your work?' Lydia asked, picking her way through her risotto, her usually healthy appetite the size of a sparrow's under Anton's scrutiny.

'Most of the time.' Anton nodded. 'It does not leave me much time for myself, though…' He frowned as Lydia raised a slightly questioning eyebrow. 'It doesn't!' he insisted.

'From what I've gleaned, you've found the time to maintain an incredibly active social life, Anton.'

'It really isn't as good as the magazines make out.' Not remotely embarrassed by her inference, Anton gave an easy shrug. 'A lot of those so-called relationships were nothing more than a few dinner dates.' Lydia's eyebrows were practically in her hairline and Anton managed a wry laugh. 'So I don't like to sleep alone. I wasn't aware it was a crime!'

'I never said it was,' Lydia replied, but despite the hair and make-up, despite the flickering candlelight and the presence of this stunning man, her mind was still alert. The detective in her was carefully placing the pieces in this difficult, complicated jigsaw, and, shooting him a direct question, she carefully watched his reaction. 'What happened twelve months ago, Anton?'

Watching his face still, Lydia knew her hunch had been right—knew that she'd hit a nerve.

'Nothing.' To most people it would have seemed his recovery was instantaneous, but Lydia noted that his eyes were no longer able to meet hers. His hand reached for his glass and he took a sip as, to Lydia's trained mind, he played for time. 'Why do you ask?'

'I'm just curious,' Lydia said casually, but her mind was anything but. 'It would seem your *social life* became rather more active around then…' Momentarily she took her eyes from him. After ensuring no waiter was hovering she pushed the conversation a touch further, sure that her vague hunch was right—sure that somehow she was on the right track. 'And so did those telephone calls.'

'The two are not related,' Anton said quickly—too quickly for Lydia's liking. His rapid response told Lydia it was something he'd already considered.

'How can you be so sure?' Lydia asked.

'I just am,' Anton retorted, abruptly ending the conversation, clearly irritated by her intrusion.

The slightly more amicable air they had created was

history now and they stumbled on in silence. Pretty soon dinner was clearly over. His steak barely touched, Anton dropped his knife and fork with a clatter, screwed up his napkin and tossed it onto the table.

'You walk me back now?' He gave a tight smile, and Lydia wasn't sure if it was an apology for his bad English, or the embarrassment of his date looking out for him.

'Do you want to go out in the gardens for coffee— or a brandy, perhaps?' Anton asked as they walked through the hotel foyer. And though it could have been mere politeness that had engineered the question, though she was in no doubt he offered the same to every woman after a meal—brandy and coffee in some delectable surrounds—Lydia had a feeling he was delaying things. She realised that maybe, just maybe, Anton was dreading heading upstairs as much as her—dreading the stuffy confines of his bedroom—even if it was in the Presidential Suite. A night in each other's company, a night denying the attraction that leapt between them, would be an almost impossible feat.

'No.' Lydia shook her head. The gardens were the last place she wanted to be with a potential hitman on the loose. 'I think we really ought head back.'

'And I think I could really use a brandy,' Anton said sharply, snapping his fingers at the young woman on the desk, who immediately made her way over, completely refusing to follow the rules that had been so carefully spelt out.

All Lydia knew was that if she didn't get control here and now then she might just as well walk away from the job—unless Anton accepted that for now she was the one in charge, then both their lives would be in danger.

'Darling—' Smiling sweetly, Lydia took his hand as he relayed his orders to the young woman, choking back a gurgle of laughter as Anton's words abruptly halted. 'I really am tired. Let's forget about the brandy and head for bed.'

It was a credit to his strength that he didn't make a sound, his expression almost bland as Lydia's hand coiled around his and, in a subtle but supremely painful manoeuvre she had learnt years ago—one that would have bought most people to their knees in a matter of seconds—pushed his thumb up firmly against his wrist. Briskly, she walked her reluctant partner towards the lifts. For all the world they looked like any other couple heading for bed. No one could have guessed the agony Anton was in as she marched him across the foyer.

'What the hell was that?' Anton glowered as the lift doors closed and Lydia's grip finally loosened. She held back a smile as he let out a long breath and mumbled a few choice words. She didn't need a translation to guess that he was cursing her in Italian as he bent over slightly and held his hand between his thighs. 'You just about broke my thumb back there.'

'And you just about broke our cover,' Lydia said sharply. 'When I say move, Anton, we move—got it?'

He didn't answer—didn't even let her go first when the lift door opened—just marched ahead of her.

'Manners.' Lydia grinned at his tense back.

'You want it both ways?' Anton barked, pulling out his swipe card to open the hotel room. 'Well, you choose, Lydia—if you want to act like a man in a bar then that is how I will treat you. Don't act all tough one minute and then demand I hold doors open for you or step aside.'

In angry silence they entered the suite, and Anton stood with his back to the wall, eyes narrowed. as again she checked and secured the room.

'Have you ordered Room Service for the morning?' It was Lydia who broke the silence with a brisk question which Anton clearly had no intention of answering. 'I need to know, Anton, because if there's going to be someone coming in with breakfast then I'm going to have to tidy away my stuff and unlock the door...' For a beat of a second she paused. 'It will have to look as if we're sleeping together—but don't worry, I'll be fully clothed!'

'I have coffee and papers delivered to the room at five-thirty,' came the surly response. 'I can cancel if you prefer.'

'No need,' Lydia breathed. 'Don't change your routine on my account.'

'Maybe I should ring down now for some ice packs and plaster of Paris. We could spend the night making a few limb splints for me, just in case I step out of line again!'

'You're being ridiculous, Anton,' Lydia retorted. 'I was doing my job.'

'I know...' A ghost of a smile twitched on his angry mouth. 'That really hurt, you know.'

'It's supposed to,' Lydia answered, but her own mouth was curving into a smile as her anger dimmed, a tiny giggle escaping as she replayed the scene in her mind. 'Are you okay?'

'I'll survive.' Anton shrugged. 'I'm not sure if it's my thumb or my ego that's bruised.'

'Probably both.' Lydia grinned. 'I'll go and make myself comfortable and hopefully I won't disturb you—just pretend I'm not here. Carry on as you would normally.'

'Suppose I want a shower?' His voice was almost defensive. 'Suppose I want to ring for ice cream and watch the late night movie…?'

'Then do it,' Lydia replied, rather more nonchalantly than she felt. 'Anton, I've slept all afternoon, I'm not even remotely tired, so if you want the lights blazing all night that's fine. If you want Room Service dropping by, go for it—just carry on as you usually would and just forget that I'm here.'

'Forget?' A tiny mocking laugh met Lydia's ears and she watched as he peeled off his jacket and sat on the massive bed, kicked off his shoes and then wrestled with his tie, loosening it enough to slip it over his head and toss it on to the floor—undoubtedly sure that someone would pick it up in the morning, that someone would untangle whatever mess he'd created.

The analogy was as welcome as the relief that flooded Lydia—he was her problem, but only for now.

This impossible, beautiful, incredibly spoilt man was only in her life for a very short while, and she mustn't forget that for a moment.

'Forget I'm here, Anton,' Lydia affirmed, and, dragging a chair to beside the bed and swivelling the night light behind it, grabbing the magazines that were thoughtfully arranged on the coffee table, she set up her small corner for the next few hours. 'Just carry on as normal—I'm here to protect you, that's all. You certainly don't have to entertain me.'

'Fine,' Anton clipped, peeling off several thousand dollars' worth of suit and dropping it to the floor.

Lydia forced herself to concentrate on her magazine—trying to read about creating the perfect eyebrow shape as Anton wandered around the room, pacing like a restless animal. He was dressed only in a pair of boxers and his white shirt now, and he had the attention span of a two-year-old—flicking on the television, lifting up the phone and then changing his mind and replacing the receiver, even rummaging through his toiletry bag and producing his razor.

'You don't mind?'

Glancing up, Lydia rolled her eyes as he held up the offending article. 'Be my guest.'

As he began shaving, Lydia stole a tiny glimpse—and immediately wished she hadn't. The white shirt had been replaced by a white T-shirt now, emphasising his broad chest. Dark, olive-skinned legs were accentuated by the navy silk boxers, and somehow Anton Santini made the simple act of shaving look impossibly sexy—dark hair flopping over his forehead, the skin around his eyes creasing in concentration, a very pink tongue poking out of his full, sensual mouth.

But even that wasn't enough to calm his restless mood. Drying his face on a fluffy white hand towel, he headed to the window and, pulling back the curtain, stared out at the night city skyline. He watched the moon drifting past the Rialto Towers, his fingers drumming on the window ledge, while Lydia sneaked a peek from behind the safety of her magazine, looking at his haughty profile, noting the tension in his shoulders, the grim set of his jaw. She decided to reiterate what she had said.

'I know it's uncomfortable for you having me here, but you really don't have to—'

'I'm not uncomfortable,' Anton broke in.

'You were pacing before,' Lydia pointed out. 'You haven't even lain down.'

'So?' He shrugged, still staring out of the window, his fingers still drumming their silent tune on the ledge, tension etched in his every feature. 'This is how I am.' He gave another tight shrug. 'I don't sleep much—is that a problem for you?'

'Of course not,' Lydia replied, returning her attention back to the magazine—but Anton prolonged the conversation.

'I want a coffee.'

'Sorry?' Lydia blinked at him—no wonder the guy had trouble sleeping!

'I want a cup of coffee.'

'You don't expect me to make it for you, do you?'

'Of course not,' Anton snapped, clearly irritated by her response. 'But if I ring Room Service, then you have to put the gun away, move your chair, make it look as if…'

'That's no problem at all,' Lydia said assuredly. 'Anton, you can ring Room Service every hour, on the hour, for all I care—believe me, moving a chair a few times doesn't faze me at all. In fact, compared to what I usually have to do—'

'I'll make it myself,' Anton interrupted, and Lydia returned to her magazine, assuming, as one would, that making a coffee was no big deal.

Unless it was Anton making coffee!

From the noise coming from the tiny kitchen area Lydia could have been forgiven for thinking he was attempting to whip up a five-course meal! Just how hard was it to flick a switch on a kettle and peel open a sachet of coffee?

'You pull the plunger out first, Anton!' Lydia

snapped, watching in disbelief as he went to pour the filter coffee straight in.

'What difference does it make?' Anton bristled.

'None.' Lydia shrugged. 'If you don't mind picking the grinds out of your teeth all night.'

She certainly hadn't wanted to interfere—if he was so mollycoddled he didn't even know how to make a pot of filter coffee it was certainly time he learnt—but his restlessness was irritating Lydia now. The sooner he had his blessed drink, the sooner he would get into bed, and the sooner Lydia would find out how to turn her pale eyebrows into something that would rival Audrey Hepburn's.

'I know what you're thinking.' Bringing over his pot of coffee and a cup, and placing them on the bedside table, Anton stretched out on the bed, propping himself up on one elbow. Even though Lydia wasn't looking at him, she could feel him staring at her. 'You're thinking that I don't even know how to make a cup of coffee.' There was a smile behind his heavily accented words, but Lydia refused to reciprocate, just stared at the blurring words before her and attempted a vague answer.

'I wasn't.' Lydia shrugged.

'Yes, you were.'

'Believe it or not, Anton—' still Lydia didn't look at him '—I wasn't thinking about you in the least. I was actually trying to read.'

'I thought you were supposed to be on guard.'

'I am.' Lydia whistled through her teeth, giving him a taste of his words from earlier. 'I can read and listen at the same time!'

'Well, just in case you *were* wondering,' Anton carried on, to his most unresponsive audience, 'I actually make a very *good* cup of coffee. But normally I make it on the stove…' The tiniest of smiles flickered on her lips and Anton picked up on it in a second. 'What is so funny?'

'I suppose you chop your own wood too?'

'Sorry?'

'To heat the stove?'

'You are being sarcastic, no?'

'Yes, I'm being sarcastic.' Giving in, Lydia put the magazine down and finally looked at him. 'It's nearly two a.m., Anton.'

'So?'

'You flew across the world last night—you were in the swimming pool at six.' At least he had the grace to blush, Lydia noted. 'And the maid's coming in at five-thirty. You really don't sleep much, do you?'

'Hardly at all.' Anton grimaced, taking a hefty belt of his treacle-coloured drink.

'Doesn't it bother you?' Lydia asked. 'I mean, I'd be a nervous wreck if I had to chair an important meeting tomorrow and had barely slept a wink.'

'I'm used to it,' Anton said, as he simultaneously stretched and yawned.

'Maybe if you cut down on the caffeine, it would help…' Lydia paused for a moment as his stretching movement offered her a rather delicious view of a very flat, very toned stomach.

'Maybe,' Anton said. 'But then again, an armed detective by my side and the knowledge that someone wants me dead isn't exactly conducive to a restful night.'

'*Touché,*' Lydia smiled.

'Actually…' He yawned again, his eyes squinting as

he attempted to focus on her, and Lydia realised just how tired he must be. Even if it had been in the utmost luxury, the man had crossed from the other side of the world less than twenty-four hours ago, had been briefed by detectives, then sat in a meeting for hours, and managed to make it to a restaurant for dinner when most people would have been asleep by now. Somehow he wore it well, but his voice was a touch slower now, his accent a shade heavier as he spoke. 'If I were at home now I would have been asleep hours ago. It's not you, or the guns or the threats that bother me—it's the hotel.'

'But it's gorgeous,' Lydia admonished. 'You're thinking about buying it!'

'No doubt I will.' Anton groaned. 'And I'll be the one to sign off on the glossy advertising that calls it a home from home for the busy executive. But how can it be home when that tiny little bottle of shampoo is always full…?'

Lydia found herself smiling at his sleepy logic.

'How can it be home when every time you walk in it's as if you have been erased—clothes hung up, the newspaper you were reading neatly folded… I'm tired of hotels.'

'I suppose after a while the novelty would wear off,' Lydia agreed, her fingers twirling her red curls, long legs stretched out. So relaxed was their conversation that she barely noticed when her robe fell open a touch. She was completely engrossed in this intriguing man.

'Can you answer me something honestly?' Anton asked, pulling back the duvet and slipping inside, his eyes almost closed now.

Lydia's guard dropped another couple of notches. Not against the danger outside—her senses were still on high alert for any intruder that might approach—but the man before her now didn't pose any danger. Jet lagged, exhausted, after an age of fighting, the only thing on Anton's weary mind was sleep.

'It depends what you want to know,' Lydia answered easily, but the smile on her lips faded, her throat constricting when he voiced his question, and her mind whirred for an appropriate response.

'When we kissed this morning, when you were in my arms, was it merely another day in the office for you?'

It was an age before she answered—weighing up her answer, truth versus a lie—but somehow with his eyes half closed, with that delicious, vicious mouth relaxed now, it was so much easier to be honest, so much easier to answer his question.

'No.' Her throat felt like sandpaper, her honesty startling her, but it was countered with relief at finally being able to admit the truth. 'It was *nothing* like a normal day in the office.'

'Good,' Anton answered softly, a small, lazy smile on his face, and Lydia wondered if he was recalling it now, was going to sleep with that scorching encounter on his mind.

'Can you answer me something, Anton?'

'Hmm?' He was almost asleep now.

'Was it just another day in the office for *you*?' She watched a lazy frown form about his closed eyes. 'I mean, I know you've had lots of…' Her voice trailed off. She didn't actually want to go there, Lydia realised. Didn't want to think about the women he treated so casually, didn't want to be associated with that formidable list of conquests. But Anton spoke anyway, his voice thick with sleep.

'I like company.' Anton yawned. 'And I hate sleeping alone, hate having time to think about…'

'About?' Lydia pushed, intrigued.

'It doesn't matter.' Anton shrugged.

'Have you ever been in love?' Lydia asked—and, yes, it was personal, but so was what they'd shared that morning. 'I mean, do any of those relationships mean anything to you?

'One did.' His navy eyes snapped open and Lydia stared into them, her breath held in her throat as she awaited his response. She knew, just knew, that her gentle line of questioning combined with his sheer exhaustion was allowing him to open up—knew she was going to get the answer to the question she had versed a couple of hours before.

'Or I thought it did, I guess. Even I get things wrong sometimes. You should have been a psychologist, Lydia, not a detective—you were right downstairs: something did happen twelve months ago. But it has nothing to do with this, nothing to do with the phone calls I have been getting…'

'How can you be sure?'

'I just am.'

'Who was she?' Lydia asked, nervous of pushing too hard but needing to know more. And it wasn't all down to the fact she was a detective—she needed to hear for herself the name of the woman who had moved this man so. A rush of jealousy washed over her as she heard the pensive note to his voice.

'Her name was Cara…'

'Was?' Lydia whispered, picking up on the past tense, berating herself for her envious feelings as she registered his pain. 'Did she die?'

'No.' He gave a tiny shake of his head and Lydia assumed that was it, that the conversation was over and already he'd revealed more than he'd intended, but Anton hadn't finished yet. 'Sometimes, though, I wish that she had.'

It wasn't the viciousness of his words that shocked Lydia, but the certainty behind them.

And she'd have loved to hear more, willed him to go on—but, exhausted, he had fallen asleep mid-sentence. Those astute navy eyes had finally closed on a world that would have left any other mere mortal asleep hours ago.

Lydia tried so hard to focus on the snippets of information she had gleaned, tried so hard to concentrate on the job instead of the man, but over and over her gaze drifted to where he lay, watching that haughty, sculptured face, gentle now in sleep. And finally, when the moon had long since gone, when the deep silent hush before dawn hummed around the room, Lydia slipped out of her seat, ready to face the moment she had simultaneously been awaiting and dreading.

Moving the coffee table to its original place, she pushed the chair back against the wall, placed her gun carefully under the pillow and unlocked the door. Dressed in nothing more than shorts and a small crop top, she slipped in bed beside him, shivering on the cool cotton sheets and awaiting the maid's entry, bracing herself for intrusion, for danger…

CHAPTER SEVEN

IN SLEEP he reached out for her.

Heavy forearms dragged her rigid body to the soft warmth of his side of the bed. For a moment she fought it, but her shivering and exhausted body gave in. She relaxed a touch as his knees pressed into the back of hers, as she felt the dust of his thigh against her skin, the idle stroking of her ribs as he edged her closer, spooning his body into hers.

It could be any woman lying beside him, Lydia reminded herself, and his response would be the same— men like Anton weren't used to sleeping alone. Men like Anton were way too used to sharing their bed. His response to her was automatic.

A soft knocking on the door had Lydia's heart pounding in her chest. To an onlooker she would have looked asleep, but the tumble of hair over her face concealed eyes that were wide open, taking in every detail of the shadowy room. One hand was underneath the pillow, its fingers curled around the gun, and her body was locked in a fight or flight response as the door creaked open. Her ears were on alert, not for a moment fooled by the reassuring sounds of cups being arranged and drinks being poured. She made sure that she could only hear one set of footsteps—that no one else was taking this opportunity to plant themselves in the room.

Anton slept on, seemingly unaware of the danger. Downstairs there were armed police, and undercover detectives, ready to watch his every move, and even if a potential attacker was unaware of the fact, it was unlikely that they would choose a visible high-profile arena to attempt an attack. It was here, behind closed doors, where an attack was more likely—and Lydia was acutely aware of that fact, knowing that whenever a staff member entered the hazard was heightened.

Stirring slightly, as if awakening from a deep sleep, Lydia repositioned herself, her hand still on the gun. She watched as the maid first opened the curtains, then headed back to the table, arranging the morning's newspapers, moving the sugar bowl an inch or two before discreetly heading for the door.

'Your coffee's been poured, Mr Santini.'

Deep in sleep, unaware of the possible danger he had been in, Anton didn't even stir, and Lydia's attention remained solely focussed on the door until it closed behind the maid. Looking around the room, she ensured in her mind that everything was in order, that nothing was out of place. Only then did her hand move from the gun, only then did she finally relax.

'We're alive, then?'

Startled, Lydia turned her head to face him, auburn hair tumbling on the pillow, a frown marring her brow as Anton, wide awake, raised an eyebrow at her response.

'I thought you were asleep.'

'I thought that was the idea.' Anton shrugged. 'But

if I'm about to meet my maker, I'd at least like to be aware of the fact!'

Wriggling from his embrace, Lydia jumped free, busying herself by sugaring her coffee. She deliberately avoided looking at him as he jumped from the bed, yawning and stretching, and pulled on his bathers.

'What are you doing?' Lydia blinked.

'I'm going for my swim, as I always do.' Anton shrugged. 'I assume you'll be joining me?'

'You assume wrong!' Lydia answered, putting on her massive white robe and slippers, then carefully placing her gun in the pocket, her fingers coiling around the cool metal. 'This time I'll just be watching—supposedly in rapt admiration.'

'Supposedly?' Anton gave a knowing smile, and without a word headed out the door.

With some difficulty Lydia feigned nonchalance, relaxing on a lounger that faced the pool's entrance. But Anton was wrong for once—there was no time to admire his toned body as he dived into the pool and started his arduous swim. Well, maybe a second or two, but the pool and gym were far busier this morning and Lydia's attention was focussed instead on the hotel patrons. She carefully observed their movements, ensuring that no one was taking more than a vague interest in the man whose life she was guarding, and it was a relief to get Anton safely back to his room.

Whatever profit the hotel might make because Anton didn't like the intrusion of a butler they would lose in their water bill. The full half-hour he spent in the shower gave Lydia plenty of time to dress, hoping that the black pants and sheer top that she'd normally go out on the town in would suffice for breakfast with Anton.

God, he was taking for ever! She spent ages on her make-up—there was even enough time to plug in her ceramic hair straighteners and attempt to recreate the sleek, glossy look Karen had achieved so easily until finally he came out. The steam following him from the bathroom made him look like an angry genie emerging from a bottle, and the collar of his robe was turned upwards, as if he were about to step out into the snow. His eyes were two slits in his swarthy face as he took in her clothes.

'I'll take you shopping later.'

'How rude!' Without Karen's magic green powder Lydia blushed an unflattering shade of pink, utterly appalled at his rudeness. Because even if her top and trousers didn't suffice, how dared he say it? Anton didn't appear remotely bothered by her angry reaction, just gave an easy shrug and turned on his computer.

'What's rude?'

'Saying that my clothes are inadequate.'

'I didn't,' Anton replied easily, then ran a lazy eye over her as she stood there, simultaneously bristling and mortified. 'But now you come to mention it…' He gave another easy shrug before continuing, 'I always buy my girlfriends' clothes—and till now not one of them has complained. I thought women liked shopping. Anyway, you were the one who said I should carry on as normal—and *normally,* if my date only had four items in her wardrobe, I'd do something about it. Not that it often happens. I'll ask Angelina to ring a couple of boutiques, so they can close.'

'Close?' Lydia frowned. Somehow he'd boxed her into yet another corner. Somehow he'd left no room for manoeuvre. Anton Santini could be as rude as he damn well liked and it was her job to take it!

'I hate crowds when I shop.' Anton smiled. 'And, given the nature of your job, so should you! What time is it?' he added, clearly bored with the conversation.

'Six-thirty,' Lydia answered through pursed lips, though she wasn't entirely sure the question had been directed at her. She watched as Anton fiddled with his heavy-looking watch for a moment, before facing his computer.

'So it's mid-afternoon in New York and night-time in Italy?'

'I have no idea,' Lydia admitted. 'I assume you're not asking because you need to ring your mother and don't want to wake her?' She expected a smart retort, but instead she got a smile, and somehow it melted her—somehow she forgave him.

'Do you want to ring down for some fresh coffee?'

'Can we go back to bed for when the maid arrives?' Anton asked hopefully.

'No.' Lydia grinned as he turned back to the computer. He tapped out responses to seemingly hundreds of red-flagged e-mails, then delivered rapid messages into his Dictaphone—no doubt Angelina would have to decipher them later—before tapping into a calculator impossibly long numbers without even looking. She could only admire his staying power. On less than four hours' sleep, Anton had dealt with almost a day's work before he had eaten breakfast.

'Do you always get so many e-mails?'

'Always.' Anton rolled his eyes. 'I hate them—people expect an instant response.' He shook his head. 'I'm sounding sorry for myself.'

'No, you're not.' Lydia nodded knowingly. 'I know exactly what you mean. Take the telephone—I hate it.'

'You hate the phone?'

'Absolutely.' Lydia nodded. 'And I dread the day we all have video phones, when you can't pretend that your flat doesn't look like a bomb just hit it when someone rings you, or that they didn't just wake you, and have to peel off your face pack... It's just so invasive,' Lydia finished weakly, but Anton was smiling now, clicking off his inbox and swinging around on his chair to face her.

'What are you going to do with yourself today?'

'Sleep, hopefully,' Lydia offered. 'After breakfast I'll come back to the room and have a shower—assuming you haven't drained the entire hotel of hot water—and then I'll crawl into bed. When I wake up I'll get my hair and make-up done, so I can look suitably gorgeous to hang on your arm for the night—it's hell being rich.'

'Do you come down to breakfast with me?'

'I'm afraid so.' Lydia nodded.

'And if I need to leave the meeting? If there is an adjournment—?'

'I'll be told,' Lydia broke in, glad that he was finally taking her being here seriously. 'If there isn't time for me to come down and meet you in the bar, or if that would look too suspicious, then just come up to your room as you normally would. One of the detectives you first met will take the lift with you.'

'Your boyfriend?'

'My *ex*-boyfriend,' Lydia corrected, unplugging her

beloved ceramic hair straighteners and standing up. 'How did you guess?'

'Easy,' Anton answered. 'It's supposed to be me he's watching, but he cannot take his eyes off you. Take it from me—he doesn't want to be your ex!'

'Then he'd better get used to the fact that we live in the twenty-first century and realise that women are capable of holding down a demanding job,' Lydia snapped.

Anton deftly swooped. 'Another chauvinist?' He raised a knowing eyebrow, and, tongue firmly in cheek, he terminated the discussion. 'My God, Lydia, the world's full of them!'

As Lydia raced for a suitably crushing response, Anton swiftly changed the subject. 'Why don't you have your shower now, then you can just go straight to bed after breakfast? I'll let the desk know and they can service the room straight away. You must be tired.'

'I am,' Lydia admitted, the wind taken out of her sails, surprisingly touched by his thoughtfulness. 'But if I even so much as step into that bathroom my hair will frizz, and any attempt to look like your sophisticated lover will evaporate as quickly as my hair serum!' Her rapid English must have been too fast for him, because from the expression Anton gave her he clearly had no idea what she was talking about. 'I'll shower *after* breakfast.'

'As you wish.' Anton nodded and went to turn away but changed his mind, clearly something on his mind. 'Won't it look suspicious?'

'What?'

'You are supposedly in Melbourne to work. If you just come back to bed—'

'After your little display yesterday,' Lydia broke in, a tight smile on her lips, 'I'm sure the staff will all assume that I *have* been working—all night! They'll be *expecting* me to crawl into bed exhausted.'

'I really am sorry about that.'

'I know,' Lydia replied, though not particularly graciously.

'I was embarrassed,' Anton admitted. 'And I overreacted.'

'I know.' This time her response was kinder. Perhaps for the first time she was seeing things from his side— the humiliation he must have felt when he had found out their entire meeting had been engineered, that the woman he had practically made love to was in fact being paid to be with him. 'Let's just forget it, shall we?'

'I'm trying to.' Anton shrugged. 'I'll get dressed, then.'

'Fine.' Lydia nodded.

'Fine,' Anton agreed.

Not for the first time an appalling awkwardness descended, the Presidential Suite diminishing in size as Anton located his clothes and Lydia turned her back and feigned nonchalance. She picked up that blessed magazine and tried reading again how to shape her eyebrows as he pulled off his robe and began to dress. She tried not to imagine that gorgeous body stripped naked, had to actually concentrate on not turning her head for even a second, and wondered for the millionth time how she was going to get through this—how she could possibly keep her mind on the job when her body screamed out for Anton.

'Done.'

'Good,' Lydia responded, placing her gun in her

handbag before turning to face him, wondering how, dressed in yet another white shirt and dark suit, he could still make her catch her breath. 'Ready, then?'

'Not quite.'

No wonder he always smelt gorgeous, Lydia thought, as practically half a bottle of cologne was splashed on his cheeks.

'I'll always be able to find you.' Lydia smiled. 'If I lose you, I mean.'

'I do not know what you are talking about,' Anton replied, raking a comb through his damp hair, then filling his pockets with his swipe card and wallet. He picked up his laptop and placed it under his arm, and Lydia noted that he didn't even check his final appearance in the mirror—but then again there was no need to. He looked, as always, completely immaculate.

'There's no greater shame in my job than losing someone you're supposed to be watching—but all I'd have to do is follow your scent, or, at worst, wave that bottle under a sniffer dog's nose. Though it would probably render him unconscious.'

'Do you always talk so much in the morning?'

'Always.' Lydia grinned, stepping out of the suite and into the corridor, having to half run to keep up with his incredibly long stride.

But despite the casual chit-chat she felt incredibly shy when they were in the lift, nervous of being back on show with him, for the act to resume… Because it had been on hold, Lydia realised as the lift swooped down to the first floor. Yes, she'd been on duty, and yes, there had been a gun by her side and a two way radio, but for a while there it had been about them—about a man and a woman mutually attracted and getting to know each other a bit better.

'Anton—over here!' Angelina waved a heavily jewelled hand as they entered the restaurant, signalling them over to where she sat with a rather pained-looking Maria. 'Join us!'

'Oh, no,' Anton muttered out of the side of his mouth. 'That's all I need.'

'Looks like you're going to have to learn how to be sociable in the morning.' Lydia laughed as Anton managed a brief wave and smile and headed over to their table.

He did no such thing! In fact Maria and Lydia were completely forgotten as an impromptu breakfast meeting ensued, with Angelina and Anton commandeering most of the table, pulling out their laptops and mobile phones, talking loudly. Had she really been his girlfriend, Lydia would have walked off in a matter of minutes, but instead she took the opportunity for a quick catch up with her colleague.

'You have no idea what I'm going through,' Maria groaned.

'Nor you of what *I'm* going through.' Lydia sighed, but, catching Maria's expression she felt a smile break out on her tense mouth. 'What's wrong?'

'Nothing.' Maria shook her head. 'Anyway, we shouldn't be seen talking.'

'Ah, we can be seen talking now,' Lydia corrected. 'Angelina called Anton and I over—we certainly didn't engineer this meeting. We're just two women who've been introduced and are having a gossip—no one can hear what we're saying. So come on, Maria, tell me what the problem is.'

'It's nothing to do with…' Maria's voice trailed off. Words like 'the case' or 'bribes' were clearly out of bounds, even if it appeared that no one was listening, but Lydia got the unspoken message.

'Salacious gossip isn't my forte,' Lydia reminded her.

'I know.' Reaching over to the bread basket, Maria selected a croissant before finally talking, her voice so low Lydia had to strain to catch it. 'They should have made us *sisters*.'

'Sisters?' Lydia frowned. 'But you're way too young to be her sister. It would have looked…' Her voice trailed off as she remembered to keep the conversation vague.

'I'm not talking about being her sibling.' Maria shuddered. 'I mean…' As Maria broke open a croissant Lydia saw that her hands were shaking. Her jaw dropped a mile.

'She *fancies* you?'

'I think so.' Maria's face was scarlet, clearly in serious need of a green-based foundation and Lydia did the only thing she could—burst into a fit of giggles. Finally, Maria joined in.

'Something amusing?' Anton glowered across the table.

'Just chatting, honey,' Lydia said sweetly, blowing him a kiss and enjoying the flicker of annoyance that passed over his face before he turned back to his computer.

'There is a glimmer of hope.' Using her serviette to dab her face, Maria let her giggles fade and she sounded like any PA's assistant from the world over as she carried on talking. 'Apparently Anton raced through things yesterday. The hotel's figures tally with his external audit, so, with a bit of luck, they'll be finished by the day after tomorrow and then they can head back to Italy.'

It was as if a bucket of water had been thrown over Lydia. The laughter that had been so therapeutic faded in an instant, realisation shrinking her momentary good humour.

'The day after tomorrow?' Lydia checked.

'Hopefully,' Maria countered, spreading jam on her croissant, so relieved to have shared her predicament she didn't even notice Lydia's rigid expression. 'And then we can all go back to our lives.'

'I'm going to the meeting room.' Closing his computer, Anton stood up and made his way around the table.

'You should slow down a touch—at least enjoy your breakfast properly,' Angelina chided. 'You work far too hard.'

'I pay you to assist me,' Anton clipped. 'Not mother me.'

'Come, Maria, we have work to do,' Angelina said, not remotely fazed. Clearly she was used to being snapped at by Anton.

As he stood up Lydia held her breath, wondering what he was going to do this time—kiss her possessively on the mouth again, as he had last night, perhaps? Remind her to get a lot of sleep because she'd be needing a lot of energy? She was sure, given his previous exploits, that he'd do something, anything to embarrass her, but she shivered inside with excitement all the same.

She was way off with her predictions—he didn't even bother to say goodbye, just stalked out of the restaurant without a backward glance, followed by his entourage. And Lydia realised, as she sat there with cheeks flaming, stinging from his dismissal, with the heavy scent of him lingering long after he'd gone, that she'd rather have been humiliated than ignored.

Swiping her card to open the door to the Presidential Suite, Lydia understood a little more where Anton was coming from—every trace of him, of them, had been erased. The clothes that had littered the floor were all back in the closet, coffee cups and glasses had been washed and replaced, the rumpled bed was made and taut. All this Lydia took in as she carefully performed her routine check, noting that even the heady scent of Anton had been erased. Opening the heavy glass bottle of cologne, she inhaled his fragrance and shivered a touch at the images his scent conjured.

She didn't want to go back to her life.

Didn't want this fairytale to end before it had even begun.

And it had nothing to do with the clothes and the hair, nothing to do with luxurious surroundings or having eager staff at her beck and call.

It had everything to do with Anton.

The real Anton—not the brash, chauvinistic version she had encountered so many times, but the deep, sensitive, incredibly sensual man she had glimpsed.

Her exhausted, sleep-deprived brain waged a weak argument.

Anton hated her job as much as Graham did.

But Anton had the guts to admit it, Lydia countered; Anton didn't hide his sentiments in the way most men did.

He made her feel like a woman. Not the weak, pale

version Graham and the men before him wanted—a woman who needed protection, a woman who needed a strong partner—instead he made her more.

More.

Sitting on the edge of the bed, Lydia buried her tired face in her hands and tried to qualify what she was thinking. More feminine, more sexy, more vibrant. He made her feel more than she had ever felt in her life. In one day and a night it was as if her life had been transformed—as if he'd dipped her in some wonderful primer, bringing out the best, the shiniest, the most beautiful qualities she held, not attempting to hold her back or reel her in.

She was literally drooping with exhaustion now, ready for a quick warm shower and hoping that it wouldn't revive her. The last thing Lydia wanted was a second wind. Her few precious hours alone needed to be used wisely, and sleep was her top priority if she was going to stay alert over the next couple of days.

The bliss of hot water on her tired body was unrivalled. She washed away the conditioner, the hair serum, the subtle yet heavy make-up, stripping away the chic woman she was portraying. Her hand reached out for the shampoo bottle, a gurgle of laugher escaping when, as Anton had predicted, it was full!

She didn't even have the energy to dry her hair—just rubbed a towel over it and then listlessly brushed it and tied it back, grateful that Karen would sort out the inevitable tangle later. After pulling the curtains and slipping off her robe, Lydia peeled back the immaculately made bed, placed her gun under the pillow, and climbed inside.

* * *

God, she looked beautiful.

Walking quietly across the room, he took a moment or two to adjust his eyes to the darkened room, to adjust his psyche to the peaceful stillness after the noise and commotion downstairs, the high that charged him at work ebbing away as he stared down at Lydia.

Quite simply, she *was* beautiful.

More beautiful than he had ever seen her.

The make-up was gone, freckles he hadn't noticed before dusting over her perfect, slightly snubbed nose. Her hair till now had always been straight, either dragged by the pool's water, or sleek from a trip to the salon, but now it was pulled back in a ponytail, wispy burnt reds and oranges spilling from the tie and framing her delicate face. The colours even in the semi-darkness were like the night sky falling over his beloved home town.

He had seen her without make-up in the pool, but now, seeing her so relaxed, he realised just how tense she had been. It was like seeing her for the first time, so young, so vulnerable, and it stirred something far deeper than lust in him—something he was scared to interpret, something that made his heart almost still in his chest for a moment. He was scared—not for him, but for her—scared at the casual price she placed on her life, the job she did, the bastards she exposed herself to in the name of duty.

Someone was watching her,

That feeling that someone was in the room, that she was being watched, had Lydia struggling into conscious-ness, like a deep-sea diver being forced to rapidly ascend.

Disorientated, confused, still her mind worked on

autopilot. Resisting the urge to snap her eyes open, she pretended to stir, her hand reaching under the pillow. It took less than a second, but it felt like for ever.

'Why,' came an angry, familiar voice, 'are you lying here asleep without the door chain on?'

Her fingers relaxed around the gun, anger overtaking her as her brain finally made the connection with the voice.

'It's not a good idea to creep up on me like that, Anton,' she bristled. 'Especially when I'm sleeping with a gun under my pillow.'

'But I could have been anyone. It is not safe, you up here alone.'

'They're after you, not me,' Lydia pointed out. 'And the door has been left unlocked so that you can come directly in—if someone *were* following you, the very last place you'd want to find yourself is locked outside your suite, knocking on the door, waiting for me to wake up!'

'I don't think it is a good idea,' Anton insisted. 'You put yourself at too much risk.'

'That's not your concern,' Lydia answered, staring up at him from the bed as he towered over her.

'It shouldn't be,' Anton countered. She watched as his harsh expression softened, watched the bob of his Adam's apple as he swallowed, those knowing eyes almost confused as he stared down at her, his usually strong voice thick with emotion when he spoke on. 'But all of a sudden it is.'

The magnitude of his words should have came as little surprise—after all, she was feeling it too—but the fact that Anton Santini was standing over her, baring his soul, telling her he was scared for her, concerned for her, was almost too much to comprehend.

'I hated the restaurant this morning,' Anton said, his voice gruff. 'Up here it's just us, isn't it?' When she didn't respond he elaborated, each word revealing the depth of his feelings, each word telling Lydia that she hadn't been imaging things, that Anton Santini felt it too. 'But as soon as we step outside that door I'm reminded again that it's all just an act.'

'Anton…' she started, but her voice trailed off, the absolute impossibility of their situation starting to hit home. They lived on opposite sides of the globe, had careers that demanded all from them, were two separate people from two different worlds, and nothing could change those facts. 'In a few days you're going back to Italy…'

'We should be finished here the day after tomorrow.'

Even though Maria had unwittingly warned her, still the words fell like a guillotine—the death sentence to their fledgling relationship.

'I fly back to Italy in a couple of days' Anton affirmed. 'I have come now to get some files that I hadn't thought would be needed today because things have moved on far more quickly than any of us expected. All we have to do now is go through some more figures, a few more presentations, then it will be merely a case of signing on several hundred dotted lines. There is no reason to stay longer.' Anton stared down at her. 'I don't think your colleagues would be too thrilled if I told them I was staying on in Melbourne for an impromptu holiday! Why don't *you* do it, though?'

'Do what?'

'Come back with me?' Anton stared down at her. 'We could spend some time together—some *real* time together…'

'It's not that easy, Anton.' Lydia almost snapped the words out, terrified that if she didn't stay strong she might give in—might lose her head and take him up on his offer. 'I'm up for promotion. I can't just take a couple of weeks off when I feel like it.'

'If you have no holiday time left I can…' Seeing her face harden, he stopped talking, but he needn't have bothered. The offer, even if hadn't been voiced, was there.

'Pay for my time?' Angry eyes glittered as she spoke.

'You are twisting my words. I like you, Lydia, and I want to spend time with you. I was just trying to come up with some way to do that.'

'You don't know me, Anton,' Lydia pointed out. 'You see this groomed, elegant woman, who's at your beck and call—a woman who supposedly has nothing better to do than sit in her room and wait for your meetings to finish. That isn't the real me.'

'I'm aware of that. That is why I want to spend time with you, and get to know the real Lydia.'

'She's nothing like this!' The words were delivered with a defiance that startled even herself. 'The real Lydia wears jeans and sneakers. The real Lydia works twelve, sometimes twenty-four-hour shifts, and she certainly wouldn't take being spoken to the way you saw fit yesterday.'

'I'd already guessed that.' A tiny smile ghosted his lips as he gazed down at her. 'And, at the risk of enraging you further, you're not looking particularly groomed or elegant now!'

Bastard!

Too livid even to blush, Lydia spoke through pursed lips, challenging him with her eyes. 'Would I suffice, Anton?' she asked. 'If I couldn't be bothered with make-up or the hairdresser this afternoon? If I pulled on my inadequate black trousers and off-the-peg top to join you for dinner, would you still want me?'

Anton didn't answer, just ran an eye over her un-made-up face and messy hair, the expression on his face unreadable. 'Come with me, Lydia. Let's get to know each other better.'

'There's no point.' She almost shouted the words, angry at the impossibility of it all, angry at Anton, too, for pretending they might stand a chance when they both knew it would be over before it even started.

'You're quite sure of that?'

There was dignity in his question—no argument, no pleading his case, no fanciful lies to attempt to sway her, just a tiny chance for Lydia to retract.

She dragged her eyes from his, staring fixedly at the ceiling, terrified that if she looked at him she'd waver. 'I can't come.'

'Can't or won't?'

'Both.' Lydia held her breath, watching as Anton's eyes narrowed. 'I can't come because of my work and I won't because…' Her argument ended there, because quite simply there wasn't one.

'You want me as much as I want you.'

Anton spelled it out to her, delivering irrefutable facts, but in a stab at self-preservation somehow Lydia managed a denial, knowing that if she gave in now, if she followed him, yes, it would be wonderful, yes, it would be divine—but it could never, ever last. A man like Anton would eat her up and spit the pips out afterwards—she'd read his bio.

She knew the score.

'No, Anton.' Somehow she managed to look at him as she lied. 'For a while there I thought I did, but no.' She shook her head firmly. 'You're not what I want.'

She watched as he opened his mouth to object, but there had been a finality to her voice that must have reached him, because snapping his mouth closed he gave a curt nod of his head, and she knew as he turned to walk away that that was that.

Men like Anton weren't rejected twice in a row.

He'd offered her the trip of lifetime and she'd refused; now she had to live with the consequences.

'I'll be back in a couple of hours to take you shopping.' He stared long and hard at her. 'Maybe you should get your hair and make-up done in the meantime.'

CHAPTER EIGHT

'BLOWDRY and make up?' Karen beamed as Lydia walked into the salon and wearily she nodded, lying back on the familiar chair, waiting while Karen transformed her into a suitable escort for Anton. 'Are you doing anything nice this afternoon?'

'Shopping,' Lydia replied tightly, and then checked herself, forcing her frozen face into what she hoped was a bright smile. 'Anton's taking me shopping.'

'Lucky you!'

She tried hard to enjoy it—tried so hard to just accept this surreal moment, to push aside the logistical nightmare Anton had created with this brief expedition. Armed detectives walked discreetly behind them as they wandered down Chapel Street and into the trendiest, most exclusive boutique that was closed to everyone except her and Anton. But even with the doors safely bolted, with Lydia able to legitimately drop her detective mode for a short while, she found it impossible to relax.

Anton had said that he wanted to get to know her better, to see the real Lydia, and then promptly ordered her to get her hair done. And now, after selecting several dresses that he considered suitable, he had guided her to the changing area—a changing area like Lydia had never seen before. It was a huge room with floor-to-ceiling mirrors, and Anton was now sitting, long-limbed and relaxed, on a leather lounge, thumbing through glossy magazines as Lydia changed again and again for him in one of the cubicles, opening the doors every now and then, utterly humiliated, parading in front of him.

'I don't like it.' Defiantly she stared at him and lied through her teeth yet again. This dress was in fact one of the most gorgeous things she'd ever laid eyes on, but she certainly wasn't about to tell Anton that! 'Anyway, red clashes with my hair.'

'It isn't red, it's more burgundy—anyway, I like it,' Anton said, as if that should be reason enough for her to want it. 'Try the grey now.'

Since their confrontation in the hotel room his mood had been wretched. Clearly unused to rejection, Anton had taken it in bad part, and had returned at his most bloody and chauvinistic, flouting the rules she had carefully laid down, demanding that she hurry up if she wanted to escort him, then walking out of the hotel with little warning, forcing Graham and John out of their newspapers and out into the street. And now he was taking out his toxic mood on her—demanding that she fit his extortionate bill, choosing shoes, perfume, even underwear for her as if she were some sort of mannequin it was up to him to dress. He was letting her know in no uncertain terms that if she was going to escort him tonight then she'd damn well better look the part.

Pulling on a crushed velvet dress, Lydia wrestled with the zipper, scowling at her reflection—furious that yet again Anton had somehow managed to choose the perfect dress, wondering how he got it so right over and over.

'Where's the assistant?' Peering round the cubicle door, Lydia called to Anton. 'I want her to help me with my zip.'

'I told her that we wanted some privacy,' Anton said, levering himself out of the couch and boldly walking into the cubicle. 'I will help you.'

This was not the plan, Lydia thought frantically as his hand met her waist and he turned her around so that her back was to him, This was *so* not the plan!

'It's on the side,' Lydia hissed. 'It's a concealed zip…'

'Oh, yes.' But he didn't move, and neither did she.

Lydia eyed his reflection in the mirror, frozen still as his hand located the tiny zip she hadn't been able to manage. He should have pulled it up. Even as she stood staring Lydia knew that by now the dress should be done up. But instead his hand was parting the soft fabric, warm fingers stealing in, softly stroking the exposed flesh. The sensible thing would have been to stop him, to push his hand away, to tell him she could do it herself or call loudly for the assistant. But quite simply she didn't want to—didn't want the feather-light strokes on her stomach to abate.

The only sound of a zipper Lydia could hear was Anton's, coming down.

'Someone might come in…' she whispered, her voice a mere croak as his hand moved lower, but Anton shook his head.

'I told you—I asked for privacy.' And what Anton asked for he got, Lydia realised. It would be more than the assistant's job was worth to come in now.

'They'll surely know,' Lydia begged, though she ached for him to go on.

'So?'

So?

The word resonated in her mind. Her body was a squirming mass of desire at his touch. She felt empowered by the knowledge that this sensual, desirable man wanted her just as much as she wanted him, and even if it was just for now, even if they could never, ever make it, somehow she wanted this moment, wanted the bliss of him inside her, wanted to follow her instincts, to take this dangerous step and finish what they'd started in the pool.

It was the most reckless, decadent decision of her life, but for now, for Lydia, it wasn't just the right one, it was the only one she could make—to go with her instincts, to heed the call of her body, to sate the desire that had overwhelmed her since Anton had come into her life.

Maybe then she'd have clarity, Lydia begged of herself, as his fingers moved in ever decreasing circles. Maybe once the frenzy he so easily generated had abated she'd be able to see things more clearly. But for now all she was could see was Anton's navy eyes, holding hers in the mirror's reflection, and transfixed she stared back at him, stared back at the beautiful man who stood behind the beautiful woman he had created.

Thoughts of the assistant waiting for them in the store, of the detectives standing out in the street, instead of horrifying her, aroused her. She could feel his hand stealing down towards her knickers, watched as he pulled the velvet material of the dress upwards and slid her knickers down. She stared at her own image, watched as his fingers parted moist, delicate flesh, and all she could see was beauty, her fascinated eyes widening as he stroked her most intimate place, the pink of her labia. And the swell of her clitoris was a sweet contrast to the angry swell of his arousal, jutting against her.

'I thought you said you didn't want me…' His fingers slipped inside, and she was so welcomingly moist, the tiny gasps in her throat so needy, it was absolutely pointless to persist with the lie.

Almost a spectator, she watched in the mirror as his other hand pushed the spaghetti strap of the dress down, watched his lips kissing her pale shoulder so deeply that surely he must bruise her. He massaged her erect nipple as his fingers still worked on below, and Lydia felt herself tip into oblivion, felt her soft mound trembling in his hand, and knew she wouldn't last more than a second longer.

Neither would he, Lydia realised, and in one swift movement he turned her around, lifting her so she was slightly above him, his fingers bruising the peach of her buttocks, his mouth working the pale, tender skin of her shoulder.

She didn't have time to process the thought, didn't have time for anything as he nudged at her entrance. All Lydia knew was that she was coming, her whole body rigid as he plunged deep within her, spilling at her entrance as she dragged him in. She could see their entwined bodies in the mirror—pearly white thighs a contrast against his dark suit, her toes curling in her strappy sandals as they scratched the cubicle wall, his fingers parting her buttocks as he stabbed deeper within—and it was all she had imagined it would be and more, the most dizzy, exhilarating ride of her life.

When it was over, when she was coming back down to earth and he was lowering her to shaky ground, there was no awful thud of shame. Dragging her against his chest and pulling her in, tenderly he held her, wrapped his arms around her till she found her balance.

Maybe she should have felt used, should have burned with shame for what had just taken place. But even when he let her go his eyes were still holding her with a softness she'd never witnessed in Anton, and his mouth for once was tender as he smiled down at her.

'I'd better buy you that dress.'

'You'd better.'

It was the most heady feeling of her life, walking back into the hotel lobby with Anton, as the bellboy rushed to relieve them of their bags, her body tingling from their union, the whole world sharper, more colourful now.

'Anton!' Angelina pounced on them as they headed for the lift, followed by a long-suffering Maria. 'I need to talk to you. Some figures don't add up—nothing major, though. We can do it over coffee at the bar—it shouldn't take long.'

'Why don't you go on up?' Anton called over his shoulder, heading towards Angelina, then stilling as Lydia did the same—and they both knew why: for a tiny slice of time he had forgotten that she was on duty, truly forgotten that she was here to protect him.

'I'll stay, if you don't mind,' Lydia said, forcing a smile and following him through the foyer with Maria, wishing that it really could be so, and knowing that Anton was thinking exactly the same.

It didn't even take five minutes. In fact, by the time

the waiter had come over to take their order Anton had cast his astute eyes over the figures and nailed the problem. 'Cross-reference that figure, but I think you'll just find that someone missed a zero on the end. Not for me, thanks,' Anton added to the waiter, standing up. 'I'll see both you ladies tonight at the cocktail party.'

'Will it be very grand?' Lydia asked as they headed out of the lift and towards Anton's suite.

'Probably.' Anton shrugged, swiping his card and opening the door to let her in. 'Why don't you get your hair put up? I think it would suit you!'

But Lydia wasn't listening—instead her mind was on her job, her hand in her bag, wrapped firmly around her gun, hazel eyes checking out the suite as she entered, standing stock still, the hairs on the back of her neck standing on end as instinct told her something wasn't right.

As Anton went to breeze past her Lydia moved quickly, deliberately stepping in front of him, halting his progress, her slender frame shielding him.

'What the…?' Anton's voice trailed off as the bellboy came into view, stepping into the hallway, his black eyes meeting Lydia's.

'Would you like me to unpack?'

'Unpack?' Lydia frowned. Her breath was coming in short, rapid bursts but her voice was even.

'Your shopping bags,' the bellboy explained. 'I have placed them on the bed—'

'We'll be fine.' It was Anton talking now, taking over the conversation and side-stepping Lydia, walking past her, pressing a tip into the bellboy's hand. *'Grazie.'*

'Enjoy your evening,' the bellboy responded, nodding briefly before quietly exiting.

'What the hell was that all about?' Anton demanded once they were alone, but Lydia said nothing for a while, checking the room meticulously before finally sitting down on the bed surrounded by the pile of shopping bags they had acquired on their expedition.

'I knew someone was in the room,' Lydia answered, raking her hand through her hair. 'Anton, I don't like him…'

'He's the bellboy, for heaven's sake!' Anton flared. 'But that's not the point. Suppose he *had* been an attacker, suppose his intention *had* been to hurt me— what on earth were you doing stepping in front of me?'

'It's my job, Anton,' Lydia answered, but her response was vague, her mind still going over and over the brief encounter, instinct still telling her that something didn't fit, that something wasn't right.

'To take a bullet?' His hand gripped her arm, jerked her around to face him. 'And I'm not going to flatter myself that it has anything to do with feelings, anything to do with what just happened. You'd do it for anyone wouldn't you?'

Lydia didn't respond. She didn't have to—they both already knew the answer.

It was the longest night of her life. Dressed in the same strappy number he had taken her in, her hair skilfully put up by yet another hairdresser Anton had summoned to the room, Lydia felt her nerves jangling more loudly than Angelina's ostentatious earrings.

His simmering black mood was palpable—the incident with the bellboy had been a non-event, yet the result had been devastating. Anton had seen with his own eyes the lengths she was prepared to go to in the name of duty, and he had confirmed for Lydia what she had known already deep down—Anton would never accept her work. The tension in the suite had been unbearable. After escaping to the bathroom before coming down to the cocktail party she had checked her shoulder for the bruise his weighty kiss must surely have left and found nothing. But even if there were no visible signs of their lovemaking his mark on her was indelible. Her whole body felt deliciously bruised, Anton's touch still reverberating through every tender muscle. Eyeing her unfamiliar reflection carefully in the mirror, taking in the sleek hairdo, the heavily made-up eyes, the sophisticated, groomed woman who stared back, mocking over and over the trembling child inside, she had wrestled with the biggest decision of her life.

'I'm going downstairs now!'

He had summoned her with a sharp knock on the bathroom door, told her in no uncertain terms that if she intended to join him she'd damn well better come now.

And—because it was work—she'd complied.

Now, watching the room, Lydia sipped at yet another fake daiquiri as Anton held court—easily a head above the rest. And though he listened intently to the conversation in progress, occasionally smiled as the people around him loudly laughed, his aloofness, his air of superiority had never been more evident.

All Lydia knew was that she didn't want it to end—didn't want to go back to the world she had inhabited just a short while ago. And it had nothing to do with the jewels and the clothes. Nothing to do with the sumptuous surrounds and the lavish wealth that swathed her now. Instead it had everything to do with the man who had transformed her life the second he had stepped into it—the man who, quite simply, had taken her heart the second she had laid eyes on him.

'You're quiet,' Maria observed as they stood on the outskirts of the entourage. 'Not that I blame you—I'm just about dying with boredom. Even when they're not working, it's all they talk about. I don't know how Anton manages to retain all those figures. He's like a human calculator.'

She so ached to confide in her friend. Not to find an answer—Lydia knew there wasn't one—but for some moral support. But now was neither the time nor the place. 'How's your boss?' Lydia asked instead.

'Like my dog when it's on heat!' Maria's mouth twitched as she took a sip of her drink. 'I should be armed with a stick to keep her at bay. Not that I'm complaining. I'm having the best time really—I've booked myself in for a hot stone massage tomorrow, which sounds divine! And so is he…' Maria breathed as Anton looked over in their direction and started to make his way over.

'Maria,' he gave her a curt greeting before facing Lydia, 'I'd like to go back to the room.'

A bucket of champagne was cooling in a silver bucket, and as Lydia closed the door behind them Anton opened the bottle with ease.

'Lock the door,' Anton said, pouring two glasses and offering her one, frowning as Lydia shook her head.

'I'm not supposed to drink alcohol on duty.'

'You had three strawberry daiquiris downstairs,' Anton pointed out.

'Which were made by one of my colleagues.' Lydia gave a tight smile. 'They were non-alcoholic, to ensure that I'm able to keep my mind on the job.'

'You weren't exactly concentrating this afternoon…'

'The shop was secure…' Lydia swallowed hard. 'But you're right. That wasn't my finest career moment. But my work *is* important to me Anton…' She watched his face darken.

'It's too dangerous.'

'It's who I am.'

'No.' He shook his head firmly. 'I saw the *real* Lydia this afternoon.'

'No, Anton,' Lydia said softly. 'You've never met the real me.'

'Come here,' Anton said softly, and Lydia knew that it was now or never, knew that he was testing her. If she joined him in his bed then he'd expect her to join him in his life, and Lydia knew that she couldn't do it. A night in Anton's arms, being held by him as she slept, seemed far more intimate somehow than what they had already shared. It would make the inevitable loss that would follow greater somehow if she glimpsed his tender side.

'Come to bed, Lydia.' It was practically an order, and it took a supreme effort to defy him, to pull over the chair and resume her guard.

'You go to bed if you want, Anton. I'm working.'

CHAPTER NINE

'ANYTHING from Angelina?' Lydia asked as Maria closed her eyes and rested back on the wooden slats of the sauna wall. Both women were delighted to be able to drop their guards for a few minutes—the only reminder they were detectives were the pagers nestled in their bathrobes that would trill if they were needed.

'Nothing—she's safely tucked up in the salon, getting her beard waxed, with Graham beside her.' Maria let out a gurgle of laughter. 'He's having a facial and a manicure, can you believe? Strictly so that he can watch Angelina while we catch up, of course, but I think he's enjoying it just a bit too much—maybe *that's* why you really broke up.'

'You're obsessed!' Lydia laughed.

'No, I'm not.' Maria sighed. 'You're looking at the new laid-back me, courtesy of the hot stone massage—Lydia, you simply have to try it. They place these warm stones all over you and wrap you up in this little cocoon, and when you're cooked, when you think you could never be more relaxed in your life, they oil you and massage you with the stones—it's bliss—sheer bliss. I swear, nothing will ever faze me again—not even

Angelina and her none too subtle advances. I couldn't be more relaxed!'

'Any news on the background check for that bell-boy?' Lydia asked.

'Nothing out of the ordinary.' Maria yawned. 'He's a backpacker who's worked for the hotel a couple of months. No criminal history…'

'Where's he from?'

'Florence,' Maria answered. 'Well, that's the last address they've got on him—and given Anton's from Sicily, and works mainly in Rome, there's nothing suspicious there. They're still running checks, but it doesn't look as if he's involved in this.' Maria gave a lazy shrug. 'I'd forget it if I were you, Lydia.'

'I don't like him,' Lydia insisted. 'Tell Kevin I want them to keep looking in to him.'

'No problem.' Maria nodded.

'Anton wants me to go back to Italy with him.'

Lydia blurted the words out, watching as Maria's eyes peeped open, a tiny frown puckering on her newly relaxed brow as she eyed her agitated colleague. 'He wants me to join him there for a holiday.'

'He wants *you* to join him!' Maria gaped.

'Is it really that unbelievable?' Lydia snapped.

'Of course it is.' Maria shook her head as if to clear it. 'Lydia, this is *Anton Santini* we're talking about. And you're telling me that he wants to whisk you away for a holiday! What on earth did you say?'

'No, of course.' Sitting forward on the bench, Lydia raked her hands through her rapidly frizzing hair. 'If I take a few weeks off to jet to the other side of the world I can practically kiss my promotion goodbye—my career, too, probably! I mean—' Lydia's hands flailed like windmills as Maria listened intently '—Graham was offering me marriage and I said no. Why on earth would I give everything up for a fling with Anton?'

'Why are you so sure it would be just a fling?' Maria asked.

'Because flings are what Anton does best—the man's a serial flinger!'

'Is there such a thing?' Maria grinned.

'I don't know,' Lydia admitted, reluctantly smiling back. 'But there should be—it should be listed in the dictionary and when women look the word up there should be the name *Anton Santini* written beside it!

'It could never work,' she added, even though Maria hadn't asked. 'I mean, just look at his reputation! And he's made it very clear he hates my work. He doesn't even know me—he *thinks* he knows me,' Lydia carried on, talking nineteen to the dozen as Maria sat patiently listening, 'but he doesn't. I'd be an idiot to go.'

'Then don't,' Maria said, closing her eyes and sinking back into relaxed oblivion. 'Just chalk it up as one of the nicest offers you've ever had! And be grateful that you didn't lose your head and do something daft like sleep with him.'

Lydia sat back on the bench beside Maria, closing her eyes and dragging in the hot air, her silence speaking volumes.

'Lydia!' It was Maria who was agitated now, the warm volcanic stones a distant memory, staring at her friend, aghast. 'Tell me you didn't sleep with him!'

'Well, we didn't exactly sleep…' Lydia grimaced.

'But you've only know him a couple of days,' Maria wailed.

'That's a bit much, coming from you,' Lydia retorted.

'We're not talking about me—heavens, Lydia, it took Graham *weeks*...'

'Months,' Lydia corrected.

'Months, then,' Maria choked. 'So what the hell happened with Anton? How on earth did he...?' Maria's voice trailed off as Lydia broke down, and at the sight of her friend's devastated face Maria wrapped an arm around her. 'This isn't love, is it?'

'I think it might be,' Lydia gulped. 'But, like I said, he doesn't even know me.'

'Then show him you,' Maria said firmly. 'Show him the amazing woman you are, Lydia.'

'You think I should go with him?'

'Hell, no.' Without hesitation Maria shook her head. 'You're Detective Lydia Holmes, and he'd damn well better get used to it.' A cheeky smile inched across Maria's pretty face. 'Give him a taste of the real you, Lydia. Don't compromise yourself, and don't play by his rules. You never have before, so why start now? I guarantee that even if he leaves he'll soon come back!'

'And if he doesn't?' Maria stared at her friend and she answered her own question. 'Then it wasn't meant to be.'

Finally she knew what to do.

Back in the Presidential Suite, like a child creeping into her mother's room, Lydia faced the mirror alone. Armed only with her rather paltry make-up bag, she slicked her lashes with mascara and rubbed some gloss on her full mouth. She tamed her wild curls with some mousse, and pulled her long red locks into some sort of acceptable shape. If Anton thought she was dressing down then he was wrong, she was actually dressing *up*.

Nerves truly hit her as her pager buzzed, alerting her that the meeting was nearing its end and to head downstairs in fifteen minutes.

It would have been so very much easier to pull on one of the dresses Anton had chosen for her, to dab her pulse-points with the expensive perfume he had bought and to strap on the perfect new shoes that lay nestled in tissue paper, courtesy of their shopping expedition, but it wasn't her.

Flicking through her wardrobe, Lydia bypassed the expensive designer gowns, settling instead on her own faithful black dress—the one staple in every woman's wardrobe. It was the same black dress she had worn for the police Christmas party, the same black dress that had seen her through plenty of first and last dates—the one dress she felt good in. Slipping it over her head, Lydia fiddled with the zip and then pulled on a pair of her own high strappy sandals. Rummaging in her handbag for her own scent, Lydia dabbed it on, her hands shaking so much she spilled most of it.

'Calm down, Lydia,' she scolded herself, placing her gun in her bag and heading for the door, stopping for just a moment to check her reflection.

And her nerves disappeared. A strange relief flooded her as she witnessed the familiar reflection, and even if she wasn't quite as elegant, quite as exquisitely packaged as she had been, somehow it felt right, it felt real, it felt honest.

Tonight she would face him as the woman she was.

Closing the door behind her, she headed for the lift, pushed the call button and stepped inside, shaking her curls, straightening her shoulders. She was on duty now, bracing herself for any eventuality, ready to face whatever tonight might bring.

Only it wasn't the thought of a security breach or the fact that her life could be in great danger that terrified her. It was the thought of Anton's reaction that caused her stomach to tighten, her throat to constrict as she stepped out of the lift and walked across the sumptuous foyer, heels clicking on the marble tiles…

Anton's reaction when he saw the real Lydia.

'Lydia!' Draped in some hideous multi coloured kaftan, Angelina summoned her over while simultaneously ramming tiny slivers of pâté-drenched toast into her mouth. 'You look fantastic—love the hair. Did you have a perm? What a brave move!'

'Thanks.' Lydia forced a smile, and then shook her head as Angelina thrust a glass of champagne at her.

'No, thanks, it gives me the most appalling head-ache.' Glancing over at the bar, she checked that Kevin had seen her arrival before summoning a waiter. 'I'd like a strawberry daiquiri please. Extra sweet,' Lydia added, then waved a finger in Kevin's direction. 'He knows how I like it.'

'Certainly.'

'Where's Anton?' Lydia asked Angelina, happy that her drink order had been taken care of.

'He's just signing some papers—he should be out soon,' Angelina said, summoning back the waiter Lydia had just spoken to and exchanging her empty champagne glass for a full one.

Lydia was grateful for the momentary reprieve and turned with a beaming smile to Maria, kissing her on the cheek.

'You look fabulous!' Maria said.

'Really?'

'Really.' Maria grinned. 'You'll knock his hundred-dollar socks off!'

'We've done well.' Angelina was back, draining her glass in one gulp. 'The deal is finalised, so tonight we can party before we head for home.'

'Or maybe we can get some sleep!'

His dry, deeply accented voice practically sent her already shot nerves into orbit. Her spine tensed as she felt the heat of his hand on the small of her back, radiating warmth through her dress, and, turning her cheek, she closed her eyes for a second, relishing the dizzy brush of his lips against her cheek as he joined the gathering.

'You look stunning.' His low tones were for her ears only, and, carrying on the intimate mood, she turned to face him. 'Stunning,' he said again, his eyes dragging over her face as if slowly taking in each freckle, lingering on her full lips, the riot of curls that framed her face. 'Your hair's amazing—did someone new do it?'

'Yes.' Her eyes glittered back at him, taking in every flicker of his reaction as she delivered her words. 'Me.'

It was only the two of them. Angelina's loud voice faded, the crowd, the waiters seemingly melted away, leaving just the two of them facing each other. 'I did my own hair and make-up—this is me you're seeing, Anton.'

'Hello, you.'

Two little words, husked from his lips. His mouth had barely moved as he spoke, but one hand reached up to her hair, catching a heavy ringlet and coiling it around his finger in a curiously possessive gesture. His eyes ravished her, caressing each feature, taking in the almond-shaped eyes, the delicate snub of her nose, as if truly seeing her for the first time.

'Will *you* join me for dinner?' He offered his arm, clearly certain she would accept, a quizzical smile on his lips as she slowly shook her head.

'No, Anton, will *you* join *me*?'

'Where?'

And she'd have loved to take him by the hand, to lead him away from the grandeur of the hotel and out into the hustle and bustle of Melbourne's streets, to show him her favourite restaurant and later, to wander hand in hand along the river—would have loved, even more, to take him to her home.

To invite him in for coffee, so to speak.

But this was the strangest of first dates, and protocol didn't allow such luxuries.

A wry smile twisted her lips at the incongruity of her thoughts—they were, after all, in practically the most luxurious hotel in Melbourne, with a legion of staff to attend to their every whim, their every need, but right now true luxury would be her own little flat and Anton. There would be no one watching, no guidelines to follow, no conversations to steer. Just the sheer, decadent luxury of being truly together.

But instead she invited him to the one other place they could be themselves—the one place they could really let down their guard and talk without fear of being overheard.

'I've ordered food to be delivered to the room.' Her voice was so low he had to lean forward to hear her, his cheek dusting hers as she leant in and spoke. 'I thought perhaps we could talk…' She gave a tiny nervous swallow, trying to summon up the courage to lay down some guidelines. 'Talk,' she said again. 'Get to know each other a bit more. If you still want to, I mean.'

'There's nothing I want more,' Anton said solemnly, but his mouth twitched in a small private smile. 'Well, one thing, perhaps. But there are things we need to take care of first, yes?'

'Yes.' Lydia nodded, sharing his smile with one of her own, but blushing as she did so.

'I'll go and say my farewells, and then…' His eyes held hers. 'Then we will spend some time together, Lydia.'

'Is everything okay?' Maria cornered her as Anton made their excuses, spoke to his colleagues and bade them farewell for the night.

'Everything's fine. Anton wants to have dinner upstairs in his room,' Lydia said as lightly as she could. 'And I have to admit I'd be a lot happier away from the crowd.' Even though no one appeared to be listening, still Lydia chose her words carefully. But Maria got the thinly disguised message, delivering a tiny encouraging wink in her friend's direction.

'I just hope to God Angelina doesn't get ideas and suggest an early night herself. Frankly, I'd rather take my chances down here!'

'I don't think you need to worry.' Lydia smiled, watching as Angelina monopolised another drinks waiter. 'A couple more champagnes and she'll be out like a light!'

CHAPTER TEN

'HAVE YOU changed your mind about coming to Italy with me?' Anton asked when finally Lydia had checked the room and placed her gun on the bedside locker, when finally they were truly alone.

'No.' She faced him, revealing a little more of herself that perhaps he didn't know. 'I don't change my mind very often, Anton.'

'Neither do I.'

And it could have been checkmate—two proud, stubborn people unwilling to make the first move—but for now Lydia wasn't thinking about tomorrow. Instead she was thinking about the here and now, revelling in what they had, determined to enjoy the moment.

'What's this?' Frowning, he watched as Lydia lifted the heavy silver lids on the table, revealing two white boxes and a brown paper bag already shiny from its greasy contents. 'Noodles?'

'Not just any noodles,' Lydia corrected. 'The best noodles in Melbourne—when I'm on night shift I always grab a box, and generally there's enough left over for breakfast in the morning. I had them delivered, then asked the chef to heat them up—I don't think he was very impressed.'

'And these?' Anton peered into the brown paper bag.

'Spring rolls.'

'Not like any I've ever seen.'

'Try one,' Lydia said, sitting down at the table and smothering a smile at the role reversal. Anton was staring at the cheap wooden chopsticks, clearly used to working cutlery from the outside in. 'They pull apart.'

'So they do.' Anton grinned, and with enviable ease worked his way through the noodles. It was the most wonderful meal of her life—the food divine, the conversation easy. They were getting to know each other a little better, laughing at each other's jokes, finding out what made the other tick.

'The chef would have a coronary if he could hear me—but that was an amazing meal.'

'I told you so.' Lydia smiled, but it was short lived. The light-hearted conversation that had filled the room was fading as the seriousness of their situation hit home.

'So you're not coming?'

'No.' Lydia shook her head.

'Then how…?' Anton started.

'I don't know.'

Crossing the room, he took her in his arms, held her so fiercely, so closely, that for that moment the problems they faced barely mattered. All she could feel was him, and it felt so right it hurt. The cradle his solid arms provided comforted her, his masculinity enhanced her femininity. His arms swathed her, holding her so close, their roles easily reversed—Anton the protector, Anton trying to tell her that it would all be all right, that some-how they could make it work.

'Would it make things easier if I gave some sort of commitment…?' His English was faltering but his in-tention was clear, and Lydia pulled back from his em-brace.

'A diamond isn't going to solve this, Anton,' Lydia said. 'It isn't that easy. But let's not think about it now…' Leaving the warmth of his arms, she headed for the door and double checked it.

'What are you doing?'

'Making sure it's secure.' There was a tiny tremble in her voice, her simple answer loaded with complicated meaning as she moved a chair and wedged it firmly in front of it. 'So I don't have to watch it.'

'The maid comes in at—'

'I already cancelled,' Lydia said, because he made her feel bold, made assertion possible, because finally she had found in a man what she needed. A man so com-fortable in his own skin, so confident in his own abili-ties, his own sexuality, that he wasn't threatened by hers. She turned and faced him. The doubts, the ques-tions in her mind were still there, but despite the internal wrestling, despite playing over and over the worst case scenarios of losing him in her mind, one constant re-mained—she wanted this night with him.

'Come here,' Anton said softly, using the same two words that had enraged her just a few days ago. But he was summoning her to his bed now, not his table, and his voice was so thick with lust, his eyes so loaded with desire, there was no question of feeling humiliated. Actually, Lydia realised, there were no questions at all in her mind—just want and need, propelling her those last few steps to his bed.

Her nerves caught up with her just a touch as he pulled back the bedlinen and, taking her trembling hand, guided her towards him. He held her close for a moment, the gesture somehow reassuring, stroking her long slender neck, the nub of his index finger exploring the pulsing hollows of her throat, then working down, slowly down, tracing the rigid prominence of her clavicle as his mouth finally found hers.

He undressed her slowly, savouring every slip of the fabric with his tongue, and with every kiss, every tender word he made her feel beautiful, feminine *and* beautiful—which sometimes was the hardest thing in the world with a job like Lydia's. No matter how fit, how assertive, or how much she craved the adrenaline and the danger of her work, sometimes all she wanted was to feel like a woman. And Anton achieved that just by looking at her.

There was no haste in his movements, no hurried gestures, so blatant, so potent was the chemistry between them. Long, deep kisses that made everything okay, made everything suddenly all right, giving her the impetus to undress him, her trembling fingers working the buttons of his shirt, Anton helping her, until for the first time they faced each other naked.

Quite simply he was more beautiful than even her mind had allowed, and the giant step to his bed was easy now, desire guiding her as he laid her down beside him. His fingers caressed the pale flesh of her breast and she could feel it swell in his hand, warm to his divine touch, to his finger slowly, slowly stroking her nipple, drawing it out to its needy length as still he kissed her. All Lydia could do was shiver at his skilful touch—submit to the pleasure he so easily generated. His touch was electric on her cool skin as he connected again the unbreakable circuit he instigated with one flick of his hand. And though her exposed body craved his touch he made her wait, taking a long, decadent moment to admire her naked beauty, slowly taking in every intimate feature, from the riot of titian locks on the pillow down to the golden curls that covered her womanhood.

She should have felt horribly exposed, should have felt embarrassed, but instead under his adoring gaze she felt beautiful. Her eyes closed in unbridled pleasure as his lips lowered to her chest, tracing with his tongue where his fingers had been. His hand was still moving, but to a far more intimate place, sliding into her needy warmth. Tiny gasps escaped from her throat as his fingers moved slow and rhythmic on her hidden jewel. His tongue was hot and teasing on her swollen breasts, his legs scratched as he parted her taut thighs with his own, cupping her buttocks in his hands, and his heated length plunged into her, filling her exquisitely.

Long, deliberate strokes consumed her, his body gliding against hers, tension meeting tension, no give, no time to relent. They were utterly absorbed, taking their time this time, revelling in the feel of each other's bodies, locked in delicious union, moving to a beat of their own, to the grind of his hips against hers. She could feel her legs shaking, her neck arching backwards, a flush of heat spreading along her spine, and she gave in then—gave in because she had no choice. Her whole body trembled as he came deep within her, as he called out her name, and her own contractions pulled him in deeper, dragging each precious drop from him until there was no more to take and he had nothing left to give.

Spent, exhausted, but still deep inside her, Anton rolled them onto their sides, his eyes never leaving hers, not even attempting words as their flushed bodies came down to earth together, knowing, just knowing, the pleasure had been entirely mutual.

'I'd better get up,' Lydia whispered, but Anton wouldn't hear of it.

'The door's locked and the chair's against it. No one can get in without us hearing.'

No one could, Lydia realised, relaxing in his arms, allowing herself to enjoy the remains of what might well be their last night together. And if their lovemaking had been divine, then falling asleep in his arms, being held by him, was a feeling that was unsurpassed.

'Anton?' Lifting her head, blinking at the harsh morning sun, Lydia heard his low grumble, felt his arm try to pull her in closer as she tried to pull away. But she wriggled free, smiling as he struggled to wake up. His body slowly stretched beside her, though his muscular legs wrapped her tighter, and she revelled in the warm, intimate cocoon of their entwined bodies, gazing down unashamedly as his navy eyes attempted to open—a sharp contrast to the sudden awakening of yesterday. 'Your plane's in a couple of hours—we ought to think about getting up.'

'It's ages yet.' Anton yawned.

'No,' Lydia corrected. 'It's almost ten.'

'No—' Anton started, but after he'd squinted at his

watch the evidence was irrefutable. 'I never oversleep,' Anton said in disbelief.

'You do now,' Lydia whispered, not even resisting as his arm wrapped around her again, jumping as the cool metal of his watch met the warm skin on her back.

'Come here.'

As he drew her back into his embrace Lydia relented for a moment, truly meaning to get up in just a couple more minutes. Her cheek was now back where it had been so comfortable, on the firm cushion of his chest, and, indulging her senses, she let him hold her. The slow, rhythmic thud of his heartbeat in her ear hastened a touch as one lazy finger circled the silk of jet hair that whirlpooled around one dark mahogany nipple, as the pad of her finger kneaded the small area of flesh. She felt it stiffen beneath her touch as the divine scent of him filled her nostrils; the last husky note of his cologne had disappeared, leaving in its place a headier, tangier, more sensual scent—the lusty fragrance of shared intimacy, *their* shared intimacy.

Schedules didn't matter any more, and her last sense was indulged as she moved her mouth a few delectable inches, her hair draping his chest, hungry lips dusting his chest, her tongue searching for the hard pad of flesh her fingers had created, lips tasting his delicate flesh.

A low, throaty moan escaped him as her lips worked their magic. She was bold now, empowered by the desire she had instigated, and her thigh moved seductively against his. The scratching warmth of his leg was against hers, deepening her arousal, and, gently straddling his body, she felt his morning glory swelling against the soft warm flesh of her inner thigh. She lowered herself a fraction to accommodate it.

Amber eyes on navy, she slid down that delicious length. And eyes closed in mutual bliss as the sweet warmth of her vice-like grip filled them—how easy it was to be herself with him inside her, to move her body against his, to *know,* just know that their pleasure was mutual.

Their lovemaking was slower now, they were taking their time because they'd only just been there, and there was no rush as she climbed that decadent hill. His fingers pressed into the flesh of her buttocks, his cool tongue exploring her, tasting her sweet flesh, biting on her fruit as she moved above him, gliding over his silken body—coveting him even while possessing him. It would have been so easy to lose herself to the moment, so easy for Lydia to let Anton take her ever higher, but the sound of her pager vibrating on the bedside table broke the moment.

Lydia grimaced at the intrusion and Anton tried vainly to ignore it.

'I have to get it.'

'You don't,' Anton grumbled, but the moment was gone.

Lydia moved across the bed and, locating the offending article, punched numbers into her phone, rolling her eyes as Anton did the same.

'John and Graham are on their way up.' Lydia's voice was flat as she pulled on her track pants and struggled with the clasp on her bra. 'You'd better get dressed.'

'So had you,' Anton whispered, taking over the bra, deft fingers finding the tiny metal clasp. He planted a kiss on her shoulder as Lydia leant forward to retrieve her T-shirt and asked, for what Lydia knew was the final time, 'Will you come?'

Picking up her T-shirt, Lydia pulled the cotton over her head, welcoming the fact that as she asked the most difficult question of her life her face was covered.

'Will you stay?'

The lift must have just been serviced, because it seemed a matter of seconds before someone knocked at the door. Peeping through the spyhole, Lydia could feel the time that had been theirs escaping like air from a leaking balloon.

'Get rid of him,' Anton said. 'And then we'll talk.'

As Anton headed for the bathroom Lydia let in her dark-suited colleagues, listening intently as they brought her up to date.

'Where is he?' Graham asked, his eyes working the room, taking in the rumpled bed, and Lydia spoke quickly to distract him.

'He's in the shower.' She feigned a shrug.

'Well, his flight leaves in just over an hour. He'd better step on it.'

'I'm not his keeper,' Lydia pointed out. 'He doesn't seem in any hurry to catch the plane.'

'Well, he needs to be,' John Miller said sharply. 'At midday his protection ends, so the sooner we get him to the airport and on his plane the better!'

'What's going on?'

Her throat thickening, Lydia watched as Anton emerged from the bathroom, rubbing his hair with a massive white towel, feigning surprise at the intrusion.

'Problem?'

Voicing the question, even dressed in a bathrobe, he was still the one in control.

'On the contrary, sir.' Graham cleared his throat.

'Things have gone extremely well: the conference has passed without event and we've got a car waiting to take you to the airport.'

'Sorry?' Anton frowned, but Lydia knew that despite his slightly confused expression he had understood every word. 'I wasn't aware that I *had* to check out—in fact, given that I practically own this hotel, I would have thought I would be most welcome to stay on here for a few days and actually *see* a bit of the place.'

'It's not that straightforward…' Graham attempted, but John Miller stepped in, his tone slightly more authoritative than Graham's.

'The security threat would seem to have passed—your stay has gone off without a hitch—'

'Maybe there *was* no security threat.' Anton glowered.

'Maybe there wasn't,' John admitted—but, refusing to be intimidated, he soon rallied. 'Or maybe someone got wind of the massive security operation that was underway and thought twice. But until you're out of the country we can't completely relax—'

'So it would be easier for you if I leave?' Anton interrupted, cutting straight to the point in his brutal, direct way.

'Yes,' John admitted, without apology. 'It *would* be easier for us if you leave. We've arranged a car to take you to the airport now, sir. We'll provide security for you till you're safely on the plane.'

Still rubbing his hair on a towel, Anton didn't seem in any hurry to go anywhere, and he certainly didn't look like someone who was about to pack his bags on command. But John Miller stood firm.

'We'll meet you downstairs in fifteen minutes; the bellboy is on his way up now to collect your things, so I suggest you get packing.'

'You were saying?' There was a wry smile on Anton's face once they were left alone. 'I don't think I have much choice other than to leave, Lydia.'

'I know.'

Sitting down on the rumpled bed, raking a hand through her hair, Lydia let out a long breath, watching as Anton peeled open a massive leather suitcase and started throwing things inside. Divine, superbly ironed shirts were given the same treatment as socks, tossed into the suitcase with no thought for the journey. No doubt he would be happy to let someone else unpack for him when he arrived in Rome. She watched with mounting despair as he walked around the room, erasing every trace of himself—tightening the stopper on his cologne and throwing it into a toiletry bag, gathering cufflinks and comb and putting them in his case. His progress was interrupted by a knock on the door, and Lydia moved to the bed, her hand edging under the pillow to feel for her gun as Anton peered through the peephole.

'It is the bellboy,' Anton informed her, and waited for Lydia to give the nod before he opened the door.

'I'm not quite ready,' Anton informed him. 'You'll have to come back—I'll ring down when I'm ready for you.'

'I can pack for you, sir.' Lydia could hear the conversation taking place, could feel the whole world pushing her to make a decision. These last, vital minutes alone with Anton were slipping away. 'I was told there's a car waiting for you and to bring your belongings straight down.'

'Fine,' Anton snapped, clearly not remotely impressed with Detective Miller's haste to get him to the airport. 'My suits need to be packed—there is a holder…'

'I'll find it, sir.'

'And my shaving stuff,' Anton added, and as the bell-boy set to work he crossed the room back to Lydia and resumed the conversation. 'Talk to me Lydia,' he insisted. 'Tell me what you are thinking?'

But it wasn't that easy. Unlike Anton, who was so used to endless staff attending to his needs that he could probably carry on making love while a maid opened the curtains, Lydia felt incredibly uncomfortable revealing her feelings with anyone else present. She was acutely aware of the bellboy's presence, and despite Kevin's assurances she was still wary of him. She watched his every move as he zipped up the suit holder and gave a helpless shake of her head, her eyes gesturing the reason she couldn't talk now.

'Could you get my shaving stuff?' Anton asked, pressing some money into the young man's hand. 'And maybe take your time?'

'Of course, sir.'

Alone again, she faced him.

'I'm being silly,' Lydia whispered. 'I just thought if we could have a couple of days here—if I could show you where I live, the things that are important to me—maybe then…' She couldn't elaborate, couldn't paint a picture of the future without knowing if Anton wanted it as much as her.

'We can do all that, Lydia,' Anton said softly and hope flared in her eyes. 'But when the time is right…'

His voice trailed off and Lydia stiffened, her eyes narrowing as the bellboy came out of the *en suite* bathroom.

'You could always stay on here for a couple of days.'

The bellboy's voice, intruding on this most personal conversation, had Lydia's hand tightening like a reflex action around the gun under the pillow. Anton swung around, clearly appalled at the intrusion. But even as her hand gripped the cool metal of her weapon Lydia knew she couldn't use it.

The bellboy's semi-automatic pistol was already pushing into the back of Anton's neck, and, no matter how rapid her response, she knew that the bellboy's would be quicker—and probably fatal.

'In fact, why don't you ring down and tell your assistant you've decided to spend the next few days in bed with your *prostituta*?'

For the first time he addressed Lydia, shouting his orders as he kept the gun trained on Anton. 'You. Over there. Sit over there.'

He waved his free hand towards the window and in that split second Lydia knew she had to comply—knew that for now she had to obey, do exactly what he said. Only when the situation was calmer could she begin to control it—from the mad look in the bellboy's eyes, Lydia knew he wouldn't have any hesitation in using the gun, and probably not just on Anton. Her hand loosened its grip on her own gun beneath the pillow, taking some small comfort as she crossed the room that he didn't check the bed, didn't remove the weapon.

'Strap her hands behind her back.' Thrusting a roll of tape at Anton, he gave more orders.

'Do it, Anton.' Lydia said firmly, determined to keep

things calm, and something in her voice must have reached him.

Anton reluctantly took the tape and bound her wrists, his hands supremely gentle, his fingers giving her just one tiny reassuring squeeze before their captor became impatient.

'Now you ring your assistant,' the bellboy spat, his Italian accent pronounced, sweat pouring down his face as he jabbed Anton with the gun, towards the telephone. 'And tell them you're staying on with your slut.'

'What the hell do you want?' Anton snarled, refusing to pick up the phone, seemingly oblivious to the appalling danger of the situation, refusing to do anything until he got an answer. 'Who *are* you?'

'Don't you even recognise your own family?'

'Family?' Anton gave a superior derisive scoff. '*You?*'

Lydia watched the nervous tic in the young man's left eye, could see the anger and hatred twisting his features. She wanted so badly to warn Anton not to inflame him, not to fuel this crazed man's anger, but even a single word from her lips could prove dangerous, could cause enough panic in their captor for him to pull the trigger. So instead she bit her lip, held in the words she wanted to say. Instead she mentally willed Anton not to antagonise him.

But clearly Anton's mind wasn't feeling particularly receptive. His mouth curled in a superior sneer as he eyed his captor with loathing. 'You're no Santini.'

'My nephew Dario is, though.'

Up to that point Lydia hadn't really been scared. Her actions were being fuelled by pure adrenaline, her professional mind too busy working overtime, assessing the situation, to really process fear, But watching the colour drain out of Anton's face as the bellboy responded to his taunt terrified her. Seeing the strong, immovable man literally pale before her, seeing the flash of panic in Anton's navy eyes, Lydia caught the first whiff of her own terror. And as their captor introduced himself further she realised that the threat to Anton had nothing to do with politics or even money, but was in fact born from the most dangerous vendetta of all—pure, unadulterated hatred.

'I'm Rico,' the bellboy sneered. 'I'm your son's uncle.'

CHAPTER ELEVEN

'THEY'RE NOT going to believe me if I suddenly say that I'm staying on.' All the certainty had gone from Anton's voice. His eyes swung to Lydia's and she saw his jaw tighten as he looked at her, saw the apology in his eyes as he held her gaze, and she knew that he felt responsible, knew at that moment that Anton was terrified—not for him, but for her. 'If I ring down and suddenly say that I'm staying in Melbourne for a few days, then they're going to know that something's up.'

'Then you'd better make them believe you,' Rico snarled.

'There's a car waiting…' Anton attempted to argue, and Lydia knew she had to step in, knew she had to calm things down—and quickly.

'Tell them you've changed your mind.' Running a dry tongue over her lips, Lydia spoke to Anton, relieved to see that Rico was nodding as she urged Anton to follow his orders. 'Make it sound convincing—if they argue, tell them it's none of their damn business. That's what you'd usually do.'

She watched as his reluctant hand moved for the phone, and knew that somehow she had to get a message out. Anton's arrogance might cause some annoyance, but it wouldn't come as any surprise, wouldn't necessarily ring alarm bells. Somehow she had to let her colleagues know that they were in desperate trouble up here. Taking a deep breath, she weighed up the risk of inflaming Rico further against the horror of being left here alone and no one even knowing.

'And tell them that we want some drinks sent up.'

'No one comes up!' Rico screamed, furious at her suggestion, but Lydia held her ground, carried on talking over his hysterical ranting.

'It will sound more convincing. Tell them you want drinks sent up but that we're not to be disturbed—that's what you usually do. Anton, you have to make them believe us. Tell them I want a strawberry daiquiri just as you would normally.'

'She's right.' Rico was nodding frantically again, saying the words over and over. 'She's right…' Waiting for Anton to pick up the phone, he gave his orders. 'Tell them to send the car away and that you're staying on. Tell them to bring up drinks, but to leave them outside. You're not to be disturbed. And you are to put the phone on speaker so I can hear the conversation.' His voice was growing louder with each and every word. 'So that I know you are not playing games! Talk to them like they're dirt, the way you always do!' Following Anton's gaze, clearly sensing his weakness, Rico crossed the room and held the gun to Lydia's head. 'Do as I say or she gets it.'

Lydia could feel her heart thumping in her chest as Anton's snobby, derisive voiced reeled off his orders— his words so coolly delivered there was no way the receptionist could possibly envisage the sheer terror on the other end of the line, no way she could even begin to fathom just how vital each word was. Lydia winced as Rico pressed the gun harder into her temple and the voice of the receptionist filled the room.

'How much longer will you be staying, Mr Santini?' The receptionist's purring voice filled the room.

'A day—maybe two,' Anton answered. 'I do not need the car—tell Mr Miller that I am grateful for his offer, but I will not be needing the car to take me to the airport. I will make my own arrangements.'

'Certainly.'

'And send up some drinks; just leave them outside— two coffees…' Lydia felt her throat tighten at his unwitting error, but thankfully Anton retrieved it easily. 'Actually, make that one coffee and one strawberry daiquiri—and make sure it is made properly, not like that poor effort last night.'

'I'll have those brought up directly.'

'And I am not to be disturbed. Is that clear?'

Whatever her answer was, they didn't get to hear it. Rico crossed the room and slammed his hand down on the phone, terminating the call. He nudged Anton none-too gently across the room and instructed him to sit.

'Hands behind your back,' he ordered.

'I might need to get the door,' Anton attempted, but Rico was having none of it.

Holding the gun with one hand, he bound Anton's wrists together with the tape, only putting the gun down when his wrists were secured and then carefully checking his handiwork. He reinforced the tape to ensure that Anton couldn't free himself, and in an appalling act of defiance slammed his fist into Anton's face.

Lydia stifled a scream, watching as Anton took the blow as if he somehow deserved it, not a sound escaping from his lips. Her eyes widened in sickening horror as she saw the jagged welt Rico's ring had left on his cheek, watched as blood poured down his face and onto his white bathrobe, and she winced as Rico's rough hands taped her ankles to the chair, and then repeated the humiliating act on Anton.

'What do you want, Rico?' Anton asked, spitting out the blood that had spilled into his mouth.

But Rico was clearly tired of talking—clearly didn't feel he needed to explain anything. He just headed across the room and sat on the bed, his gun pointing at both of them, and even if she couldn't see it Lydia could feel the hatred blazing in Rico's eyes.

The wait for their drinks to arrive was endless and the silence deafening as Rico's eyes bored into them. A thousand questions raced through Lydia's mind—questions she needed answers to. Who was Rico? Was he really related to Anton? And, most importantly of all, why did he hate him so much?

'You'll be okay.' Anton's voice was a low, gentle whisper.

'Shut up, Santini,' Rico called, but Anton wasn't to be deterred.

'It's me he wants, not you.'

Why? She didn't say it, but her eyes begged the question. She dragged them away, focussed instead on his shoulder, hoping that Anton would take the hint and not answer just yet—they needed Rico to calm down, for his agitation to abate a touch before they spoke further.

A soft knocking on the door had them all jumping. Rico shot out of his seat and stood over them as Lydia's eyes darted to Anton's. She almost wept with relief when Maria's voice filtered into the room.

'Your drinks are outside, Mr Santini.'

'Thank you!' Rico hissed in Anton's ear. 'Say thank you.'

'Thank you,' Anton called.

'Do you need anything else, sir?'

'Nothing,' Rico breathed, pushing the gun into Lydia's face until Anton repeated the word.

'Nothing.'

A tense silence followed. Rico stood rigid over them, ears on alert until finally the sound of the lift pinging told him that the 'maid' had gone. For the first time since he'd produced the gun Rico relaxed. He flicked on the television, pulled open the bar fridge and lined up the contents. He was ramming chips into his mouth, pouring spirits down his throat. Lydia prayed that he would continue, infinitely grateful that they were in the most luxurious suite in the hotel and that Anton's bar fridge wasn't the usual mini-version, but held full bottles of liquor that would hopefully anaesthetise him.

Seconds ticked away like minutes.

Minutes ticked away like hours.

As the sound of a children's cartoon filled the room and Rico laughed loudly, clearly engrossed, finally Lydia voiced her question. 'Why?'

'He's sick,' Anton said quietly. 'I've never met him before, Lydia. I just know of him.'

'Why does he hate you?' Lydia said quietly. 'If he's never even met you?'

'I know his sister.'

He didn't need to elaborate. One look at his stricken face and Lydia guessed the truth: the one woman who'd touched him, the one woman who'd got close to him, seemed to be wedged between them now, inextricably linked to this appalling nightmare.

'Cara?' Her voice was hoarse as she whispered the word, and she closed her eyes for a second when he nodded. 'And who's Dario?'

And she watched—watched as his eyes darted, watched as he paused for just a second too long before answering. And she knew, because it was her job to know, that even if Anton wasn't lying, he wasn't telling her the entire truth.

'Dario is Cara's son.'

So many questions she hadn't even voiced were answered then—such as why Rico had always spoken in English: no doubt he hadn't wanted Anton to recognise his local dialect, hadn't wanted to give Anton even a hint as to who he was.

There was plenty of time to think—to go over Rico's abhorrence of her in the restaurant, his reluctance to deliver her bags, his disinclination to leave the room that first morning. The hunch she had tried so hard to rationalise, to explain to her colleagues, was easy to explain now, with the benefit of hindsight.

Helpless, in abject misery, she watched the man who sat before her—the man who hour upon hour took without complaint Rico's demented beatings. She watched that beautiful face darken with bruises, his astute eyes become so swollen they were practically closed, trying to work out how to get them out of there safely, trying to keep her emotions in check as that dignified head tried to stay up, as somehow, despite the appalling situation, despite the appalling evidence to the contrary, each time Rico finished his vile tirades, Anton would mouth to her that he was okay; as still he tried to comfort her.

With supreme effort she pushed her personal feelings aside, forced her exhausted mind to focus, to concentrate solely on ending this nightmare, on saving the life of the man she had been entrusted to protect.

The ringing of the telephone was intrusive, and when Rico ordered Anton to answer he pulled it over to where they sat and pressed the receiver to Anton's ear. Lydia felt her heart hammering in her chest, anticipating Rico's vile reaction when he realised that the police knew of their plight.

'They want to speak to you.'

'Me?' Rico ripped the phone from Anton and his demented rage returned. He cursed into the receiver, slamming it down, and then headed for the bed. He rocked against the bedhead, the black of the gunmetal facing his nemesis, and for the first time Lydia heard him speak in Italian. But the beauty of the language was entirely lost as Rico spat out his churning, hate-fuelled words.

'Dicono che vogliano parlare, vogliano negoziare!'

And even if Lydia's Italian only ran to naming pastas she picked up on what Rico was saying—knew what her colleagues would have said to him.

'Talk to them,' Lydia implored. 'They can help you.'

'How they know?' Rico demanded of her.

'They just do, Rico,' Lydia said calmly. 'And now

you have to deal with that fact. So talk to them—tell them what it is you want.'

'There is nothing to talk about,' Rico spat. 'Because there is nothing to negotiate.'

On and on the phone rang, till even Lydia wished it would it stop. Wished that the people outside would just go away, would let her sleep, would let her close her eyes on this nightmare for even a moment.

Darkness filled the room, but Lydia knew it would end soon. Knew because her eyes were fixed on the massive floor-to-ceiling windows, her head lolling from side to side in exhaustion, her body jolting each time she succumbed. Her eyes tracked the moon on its inevitable path through the interminable night, watching as it somehow found the only cloud in the night sky and momentarily dipped behind it. That same moon had guided her thoughts last night, the same moon that would rise again tomorrow—and all Lydia knew was that she wanted to be there to see it, wanted to live her life.

'I need to go to the bathroom.' Her strangled plea dragged Rico out of his fitful slumber.

'Then go,' Rico taunted. 'Go where you sit!'

'Please,' Lydia begged. 'I have to go to the bathroom.'

'Just go here,' Anton said softly, his lips swollen, his eyes two slits in his ravaged face. 'Don't be embarrassed. There is nothing you can do.'

'Please,' Lydia begged again, noting with quiet relief that if Anton believed her, then surely Rico would too. 'I have to go to the bathroom, Rico. Please let me. It's my time, you can't just leave me sitting here…'

From her training she knew that if one thing could

make Rico weaken it was her femininity—knew that a man like Rico wouldn't be able to deal with it.

'*Periodi mestruali,*' Anton snapped as Rico's eye tic resumed. 'Let her go to the bathroom, for God's sake.'

Offering a silent prayer of gratitude, Lydia stared at Anton as Rico untaped her arms, barely registering the pain as the tape tore at her flesh, just pleading with her eyes as Rico moved to her legs. Lydia mouthed one single word—*Wait.*

Finally in the bathroom, Lydia knew she had seconds, maybe a minute to work. Eyeing the contents of the bathroom, the tools she could work with, she turned on the taps as she sat on the loo, mindful of the semi-open door, knowing that Rico was timing her.

Picking up Anton's razor, she set to work, shaving her wrists, disposing of the tiny invisible hairs, barely wincing as the blade nicked into her dry flesh, and as she flushed the loo she grabbed at one of the tiny bottles Anton so despised, squeezing a slug of hair conditioner onto her wrist and massaging it in.

'Out!' Rico shouted, bursting through the door, impatience etched in every feature. He dragged her back to the hateful chair by her hair, rough hands forcing her to sit before layering the tape around her wrists. He paused when the phone rang and, Lydia noted with relief, forgot to tie her ankles.

'Why don't you answer it?' Lydia suggested. 'Surely it can't hurt just to hear what they have to say?'

'I don't care what they say!' Rico shouted.

'If you really don't care,' Anton said coolly, his voice a thinly veiled taunt, 'then you'll answer it.'

And finally, just when Lydia was sure he wouldn't,

Rico gave in, knocking the receiver out of its cradle and putting the phone onto speaker.

'Rico!' John Miller's voice boomed over the speakerphone, imploring Rico to calm down, to listen to reason. 'We understand you're upset…'

Lydia tuned out, concentrating instead on her wrists. The hair conditioner she had applied, the smooth skin she had created, was allowing her a fraction of room to move, and hands were working as Rico swore at the telephone and knocked it back on the hook.

'Rico.' Anton's voice was amazingly calm. 'Why don't you let Lydia go and then we can talk?'

'Pay me off?'

'If that is what you want,' Anton offered.

'You really think money will fix everything,' Rico sneered. 'That fat bank account of yours will save your soul. Well, not this time, Anton.' He slammed the gun into his cheek and Lydia choked back a scream, watching as the harsh metal tore through Anton's flesh, heard again the sickening sound of metal on bone.

'What do you want from me?' Anton breathed.

'To see you suffer,' Rico answered coolly. 'No more, no less.'

'Then let Lydia go.' Somehow his voice was calm, somehow he managed to deliver the words as if it were almost a natural assumption that she should be freed. Lydia's eyes darted to Rico, fear gripping her as she awaited his response—not at the fact she might be held, more at the prospect of being freed, of leaving Anton with this crazed captor. It was a torture she couldn't fathom.

'She stays.' Rico's response was unequivocal, but Anton demanded an explanation.

'What possible good could it do?' Anton demanded, and even though his face was as white as marble, with blood streaming down his cheeks, his hands were bound and the collar of his robe was saturated with blood, there was a tortured dignity about him. His presence was still commanding, his voice firm, controlled as he reasoned with the impossible. 'You say you want to see me suffer—no more, no less. So what benefit can there be in making her stay? The police will treat you more favourably if you release her, and it is me you want after all. So let Lydia go…'

'You're not listening to me.' Rico's voice verged on hysteria. Anger and hatred blazed in his eyes as he snarled at Anton, who somehow didn't flinch. 'I said I wanted to see you suffer.'

'I heard you.' Anton's was the voice of reason but it only served to incense Rico further.

'I don't think you understand,' Rico screamed.

'I'm trying to.'

Lydia watched as Anton's eyes struggled to focus. He was squinting, fighting the pain, the nausea, the sheer exhaustion. He ran a dry, pale tongue over even dryer lips, beads of sweat forming on his brow. Not just the collar but the entire top of his robe was drenched now with his own blood, and her fear multiplied. She knew that she had to do something, that it wasn't a single bullet that would kill them both, but the slow torture of death from a thousand cuts: the pain, the injuries, the torture Rico had inflicted over the last day and night were culminating now, slowly squeezing the life force out of them.

'You have to stop the bleeding.' Lydia spoke to Rico,

trying to keep the fear from her voice, to somehow restore a strange normality. 'You need to apply pressure to his cheek, Rico—wrap something around it—he's losing too much blood.'

'Shut up.' A stinging slap blistered her cheek, but Lydia was too numb to register the pain. 'You don't know what it is to suffer, Anton Santini, so now I will tell you. Suffering is watching someone you love, watching someone you care about, robbed of their dignity, crying in pain night after night, watching Cara—'

'Speak to me in Italian.' Anton's voice cut in and sent a shiver down Lydia's spine.

'Why?' Rico's voice was a mocking taunt. 'Are you scared that she will think less of you if she knows the truth about you?'

'We will discuss this in Italian.' Anton's voice was still loud, but she heard him waver. Her terror intensified as the situation escalated, as she sensed Anton's tension—as, for the first time since the ordeal began, she saw true naked terror in his eyes. 'We discuss this in Italian because Lydia has nothing to do with this!' Anton shouted.

'Oh, but she does,' Rico said softly. 'You care about her—more than you care about yourself, more than you ever cared about my sister. And as I explained before, I want to see you suffer.'

The gun that had been pointed at her for so many hours now was out of sight, but she could feel the cool metal against her chest. The feel of the solid object pressing into her flesh didn't compare to the vile touch of Rico, the savage drag of his fingers along her cheek, the rubbing of the nub of his finger against the bitten flesh of her bottom lip.

'She is very beautiful.'

'Don't touch her,' Anton breathed, but his words fell on deaf ears.

Rico's crazed eyes bored into her as he addressed Anton. 'Tell her!' he shouted. 'Tell her how you made love to my sister—tell her how you promised you would be there for her, that you would marry her. Tell her how you cried tears of joy when your baby was born, when you held your son in your arms for the first time…'

'Rico, we can talk about this. I can explain…'

'Then do,' Rico spat. '*Explain* how when your son was sick, lying near death's door, you walked away. You told Cara that you weren't ready for fatherhood, paid my sister off with a cheque. Explain that if you can!'

And it wasn't the gun or Rico that scared her now, but Anton's response. Her eyes dragged across the room as she willed him to refute the accusations, begged him with her eyes to tell her that it wasn't true, that the man she had started to love could never leave a woman so cruelly, could never walk away from his own flesh and blood.

'I can't,' was Anton's paltry response.

'I hate you, Santini,' came Rico's menacing whisper. 'I've been tracking you since the day you left, watching your every move and waiting for this moment.'

'Why here?' Anton stared back at him. 'Why now?'

'You've caused my sister enough shame, so I'm taking care of it well away from her. You won't bring any more shame to our village, because *I'm* the one dealing with things now.'

'You're sick.' Somehow Anton held it together, somehow he kept his voice even. 'Rico, you're not well— you need help. This isn't the way to deal with things.'

'Oh, but it is. I hate you, Santini—hate the way you treat women, the way you treated my sister, the way you walked out on your own flesh and blood. I've hated you for so long now, and today I'm going to show you how much—'

'You'll never get away with it,' Anton broke in. 'The place is swarming with police.'

'Ah, but I'm sick.' Rico's smile was pure malice. 'You said so yourself. Which means none of this is my fault. How can I be responsible when I don't know what I'm doing?'

'Let Lydia go.' Anton's voice was crystal-clear. 'You're wrong about one thing, Rico. I don't give a damn about her. She's not my girlfriend—she's a police officer…'

'Liar!'

'Look under the pillow,' Anton roared. 'That's her gun you'll see. She means nothing to me, she's just someone paid to watch me. You can believe what you want, Rico, it doesn't make a scrap of difference to me—I'm dead anyway. But think about it. Think about facing a jury with a police officer's blood on your hands. I don't give a damn about her.' Anton said it again, conviction lacing each and every word.

'The same way you didn't give a damn about my sister?' Rico asked.

'The same way.' Anton met his captor's eyes.

'Rico!'

The booming voice through a megaphone outside in the hallway only exacerbated the tension. The voice that filled the room was way louder, way more invasive than the speaker phone had been, and the gun waved manically in Rico's hand as his fragile mind was toyed with.

Lydia knew that he couldn't go on much longer, that

in a short time things were going to come to a head. Furiously she worked to free her wrists, oblivious of the raw bruised skin. She rubbed them together, feeling the tiniest give in the tape, and concentrated on keeping her face expressionless as her hands worked on behind her back.

'We have someone on the telephone who wants to speak with you. If you don't pick up I'm going to play her voice over the loudspeaker.'

Rico just shouted, screaming into the stale air, every word, every action more crazed, more terrifying, more unpredictable than they had ever been.

'Rico…' The tearful rasps that filled the air stilled him, and a soft woman's voice crackled into the room, desperately urging Rico in Italian to pick up the phone, to talk to her, to end this madness. Every word inflamed Rico further. He was pacing the room now, shouting at people who weren't even there, and Lydia wished it would all just stop, wished that everyone would just go away and let her deal with it. And it wasn't Rico's response that worried her, but Anton's. She watched as the strong mask finally slipped, as thick tears coursed down his cheeks. They told Lydia without question that the woman talking was Cara.

Finally Rico kicked the phone across the room, then crouched to pick it up, and for a tiny hope-fuelled second Lydia envisaged it being over—surely Cara would sort things out? But Anton's words tore that last vestige of hope from her, and she watched in stunned silence as he addressed Rico.

'Don't pick it up, Rico. Talk to me, not her.'

'Anton?' Utterly bemused, Lydia questioned him. 'Rico surely needs to speak with his sister—'

'Shut up,' Anton's snarl was as loaded and as angry as Rico's had been, but it hurt twice as much. Lydia recoiled on her seat as if she'd been slapped, totally confused, and every last avenue seemed closed to her as Anton's verbal assault continued. 'This has nothing to do with you.'

'Yeah, shut up.' Rico sneered. 'I need to think.'

'She doesn't know *how* to stay quiet.' Anton's voice was a jeer. 'Nagging all the time, telling me what I'm supposed to be doing.'

The delirium, the paranoia that was clouding her mind, lifted a touch as she realised that Anton was somehow still in control, that Anton was trying to save her, trying to get her out before Rico finally succumbed to the mounting pressure. To free her before the appalling bloody climax that would surely ensue when Rico spoke with Cara. But Lydia didn't want her freedom— not at that price. Her job was to protect Anton, not to leave him at the mercy of this madman. Whatever game Anton was playing, it was surely the wrong one. Cara was their only hope, Lydia reasoned. The only person who could talk Rico down. This dangerous game Anton was playing would see them all killed.

'Deal with me, Rico,' Anton pushed. 'Don't listen to Cara. Don't let her talk you out of what you want to do. Deal with me, man to man.'

'Speak to Cara, Rico,' Lydia begged, shooting a furious authoritative look at Anton as she worked on to free her bound wrists. 'Don't listen to Anton. He left your sister. Why would you listen to a man who walked out on his own child?' The truth was too hard to contemplate, the words she was saying just too horrible to comprehend, but she said them anyway, knowing deep down that this was their last chance. 'Listen to what Cara has to say.'

She saw Rico waver, and though she despised him a flash of sympathy flared in her as she witnessed his pain, saw the blind confusion in his eyes, smelt the stench of his fear. And, as finally her hands slipped from the tape, Lydia knew that this was her only chance—that if she didn't do something now they were all going to die.

Lunging across the room she tackled Rico, felt the wedge of flesh against her as she wrestled him to the floor. She felt a searing pain as her head hit the floor, but it barely registered. All she could feel was the tension in Rico's hands as she fought for control. All she could hear was the release of gunshots as they whistled across the room. And then the shrill of a scream—her own scream—filled her ears as she heard, sensed, Anton thudding to the floor.

There was nothing she could do, not a single blessed thing she could do, other than go on holding Rico's wrists high above his head, refusing to let go. She didn't release her grip even as the door slammed open, even as her colleagues swarmed the room and finally secured the scene. She held onto his wrists even as Kevin held her shoulders and told her it was all over, that she was going to be okay, only letting go when everything started to blur, the shouting voices around her started to muffle.

Unconsciousness. A welcome reprieve from the pain.

CHAPTER TWELVE

'YOU'RE OKAY.' Graham's face stared down at her, familiar but strange, and Lydia struggled to place him, trying and failing to work out where in her life he belonged.

'Was I shot?'

'No.' Graham shook his head. 'You lost consciousness for a while—you had a nasty bang on your head and the doctor said that you are concussed—but you definitely weren't shot.'

'Anton?' Her voice trembled around the word. She was terrified of the answer but needed to know all the same, panic rippling through her as she again recalled the sound of the gun going off, the relentless sound of bullets in a confined space, and then worse, far worse, the thud of Anton falling behind her, the silence that had followed.

'He's fine—or at least he will be soon. They're just stitching him up, and he's getting some IV fluids…'

'He was shot!'

'He wasn't shot.' Graham sounded irritated. 'The bullet barely nicked his arm.'

'He's right.' That thick, unmistakable accent filled the room, and even in vivid green hospital-issue pyjamas he still cut a dash—even with a broken nose and a massive row of sutures in his cheek he was quite simply beautiful.

'What happened to Rico?' Lydia's voice wavered and she struggled to check it. She knew that Graham would be thinking she had gone soft, but she didn't care. Rico was sick and needed help—and, Lydia recalled sadly, the hatred that fuelled him, even if it had been appallingly displayed, wasn't entirely without reason.

'Locked up. Which is way less than he deserves. We knew you were in trouble even before you called down— some information came in that he had a psychiatric history, was actually from the same village as Santini—and we were just ringing up to warn you, calling in for back-up, when your call came through.' Graham's mouth twisted with suppressed rage. 'If it was up to me, they'd—'

'He's sick, Graham,' Lydia broke in.

'Don't ask me to waste any sympathy on him,' Graham retorted, gripping her hand, his fingers squeezing her bruised flesh. 'I thought I'd lost you for a moment there, Lydia.'

Wriggling her hand away, she stared up at him. 'You lost me ages ago, Graham.'

'Lydia…' Graham shook his head. 'You're exhausted. You've been to hell and back. In a couple of days—'

'I'll feel exactly the same,' Lydia interrupted.

And it was the easiest thing in the world to tell Graham to leave—easy because Lydia knew that she didn't love him. But as he quietly left she knew that now came the difficult part: saying goodbye to someone she would love for ever.

Impossibly shy, she gazed up at Anton, taking in the row of black sutures along his cheek, the swollen and bloodied lips and the purple bruises surrounding his near closed eyes.

'Green doesn't suit you.'

'Believe me, I don't intend to stay in them for long.' His voice grew more serious. 'You were asking about Rico?'

'I know I shouldn't care.' Lydia closed her eyes, picturing his tortured face. 'But he's sick.'

'He's very sick,' Anton agreed. 'Apparently he bought a round the world ticket and he has been watching my itinerary, getting work in each hotel I was due to visit for a couple of months before I arrived.'

'He was in Spain?' Lydia frowned.

'And New York.' Anton nodded. 'And to my shame I didn't recognise him. He was just another bellboy. Apparently he was determined to deal with me away from our village. '

And she wanted to ask why, but she simply didn't have the strength to face the answer.

'I've been on the phone to his psychiatrist in Florence…'

'Florence?'

'He moved there a while ago.' He didn't elaborate further. 'I've also arranged a good solicitor for him. Rico will get the help he needs soon.' Anton was silent for a moment and Lydia ached for him to go on, to refute Rico's awful accusations, to tell her it had been his crazed mind talking. 'Angelina's just been in. She sends you her love. She's booking my flight…'

'But you've just been shot! Surely you shouldn't even be *thinking* about flying?'

'I wasn't shot.' Anton played down his wound the same way Graham had. 'It just scratched the surface.'

Sitting down on the bed, he took her hand, stroking the pale, translucent flesh for a moment before bringing it up to his lips. Tears filled his eyes as he kissed her slender fingers. 'I didn't even feel the bullet. It threw me back off my chair, apparently, but I'd lost a lot of blood and passed out. Somehow I heard you scream, and I thought you were dead.'

'I thought *you* were!' Lydia admitted through chattering teeth. 'But we're both okay.'

'No, Lydia, we're not.' Dark eyes held hers, and Lydia knew that he wasn't talking about the nightmare they'd just been through but the one that was about to follow. Anton's voice was thick with regret. 'I'm flying to Rome tonight.'

'Tonight? But you're not well enough…' And even though that wasn't the reason he shouldn't go it was the only one she could voice right now. Her emotions were too raw for exposure.

'I'll be fine,' Anton said assuredly. 'I'll be in first class, sleeping all the way. I have to go now—there are things I need to do, things I need to sort out. I have a lot of unfinished business to deal with.'

Defeated, she sank back on the pillow, too tired, too exhausted to truly comprehend the magnitude of her loss—too damn weary to ask the thousand questions that she should be asking, just knowing it was over.

'We'd never have worked out,' Anton said, a regretful smile on his lips as he gazed down at her.

The fingers on his good hand traced her bruised, swollen cheek and she'd have loved to push him away, to tell him that he was right, that no man who called the child he'd walked out on 'unfinished business' could ever earn a place by her side, but she didn't have the strength to move. She just stared back at him, tears pooling in her amber eyes as he touched her for the last time.

'I guess you're going to have to just keep on looking, Lydia.'

'Looking?' Lydia sniffed.

'For that man who can somehow accept what you do for a living. Especially after…' His lids closed for a second, and he was visibly moved as he recalled the private hell they had shared. 'I just don't think I'd be able to deal with it,' he reiterated.

Brushing his hand from her cheek, Lydia turned her head away. 'Well, you don't have to deal with it, Anton, because I'm not your problem. Would you please just go?'

CHAPTER THIRTEEN

'READY for briefing?'

Maria popped her head around the washroom door as Lydia rinsed her face.

'Sure. I'll be there in a moment.'

As the door closed Lydia splashed her face again with cold water and then, taking a deep breath, headed to the briefing room.

'One for the ladies!' Kevin called as Lydia slipped into the room, taking a seat beside Maria. 'We've got a new pimp strutting his stuff and causing grief amongst the regulars. We're going to put an officer in under-cover—deep undercover.'

'How deep?' Graham asked as the inevitable cheers and jeers filled the room.

'Enough, guys.' Kevin's voice was serious. 'This could get nasty—you don't need me to tell you about the recent shootings. Naturally we'll have men in place, do everything we can to ensure protection…'

'I'll do it.' Maria's hand shot up and her chocolate-brown eyes darted around the room. She was clearly expecting Lydia to have beaten her to it. 'I'll do it,' she said again, frowning at Lydia's lack of response.

Somehow Lydia muddled through the rest of the briefing. Somehow she asked intelligent questions, jotted down relevant notes, even laughed along with some of the lewder jokes, but even as the group were dismissed, even as they all headed outside, Lydia knew she was going to be called back.

'Is everything all right, Lydia?'

'Everything's fine, Kevin,' Lydia responded, grateful that he was using first names, grateful that he had taken the lead and made it clear that this conversation was off the record. 'I know you were expecting me to put my hand up back there, and I know that normally—'

'You were held hostage, Lydia,' Kevin said gently. 'There are bound to be repercussions.'

'Six weeks on?' Anguished eyes met her senior's. 'It's been six weeks, and still I keep playing it over and over in my mind.'

'You'll still be doing the same in six years' time,' Kevin said, squeezing her arm in support. 'Not as much, perhaps, but it's never going to leave you.'

That was what terrified her the most. She was waiting for the day, waiting for the moment when she didn't wake up thinking about it—waiting for the day when it would all be behind her. And as much as Kevin might think he understood—he didn't. As she had with her counsellor, Lydia was keeping her pain private.

'Lydia, we all laugh in here—we all make out we're tough. But at the end of the day you were the one bound up, you were the one held against your will with a gun to your head. Don't feel bad because you can't just shrug it off. Have you been keeping up with seeing your counsellor?'

'Sort of.' Tears sparkled in Lydia's eyes but she blinked them back. 'She's very good. It's just…'

'She doesn't really get it?' Kevin offered and Lydia nodded, words failing her as she struggled to hold back tears. 'Go home,' he said firmly. 'Take the rest of the day—the rest of the week off. Take as long as you need.'

'I've already had some time off,' Lydia pointed out. 'I thought if I came back to work things would be better.'

'Are they?'

'They were for a while.' Lydia gulped. 'It's just…' She shook her head, not able to go there.

'Go home,' Kevin said firmly and Lydia knew he was telling her—not suggesting.

'And then what?'

'That's up to you,' Kevin said more softly. 'Just take your time, Lydia.'

When she stepped off the tram, even the length of her street looked liked a marathon. Dragging her feet along the warm pavers, Lydia screwed her eyes against the hot afternoon sun, too listless to cross to the other side of the road to the shady retreat of the gum trees.

She understood now.

Understood Anton's refusal to accept her career.

Understood the fear that gripped him, because now she felt it too.

But the decision that was forming in her mind, the thought of stepping down from her position, had nothing to do with him and everything to do with her.

Anton was gone…

…and good riddance.

Straightening her shoulders, Lydia picked up her feet

and walked more purposefully now. How could she ever respect a man who would walk out on his own child? She'd had a lucky escape!

Dodging the sprinklers, Lydia rummaged in her bag for her keys, trying to recall some poem she had learnt years ago in school. Unable to remember the beginning, she recalled the end, a smile forming on her lips as she replayed it in her mind…

> *To love you was pleasant enough,*
> *But, oh, it's delicious to hate you!*

And it was. So much more delicious to hate than to grieve, so much easier to hang the blame for their demise on him rather than her.

'Lydia.'

So sure was Lydia that she was imagining it, she didn't even turn around—just pushed her key into her lock and turned it, willing the images that haunted her to just go away, to leave her alone so she could get on with her life.

'Lydia.'

And she knew she wasn't imagining things then. Knew because in her dreams he always wore a suit—every image she had of him was immaculate—and yet here he stood, dishevelled and unshaven, dressed in jeans and a T-shirt, that immaculate dark hair practically unruly now, dark curls flopping over his forehead.

And never had he looked more beautiful.

'I thought you were in Italy.' Amazingly her voice was even—amazing because her heartbeat was well into triple figures. Her lethargy dissipated as she pushed

open the door and led him inside, through her tiny
hallway and into her lounge room. She watched as
tired, bloodshot eyes took in the scruffy couch she'd
been meaning to replace, the mountain of cushions to
freshen it up until she could afford to do so, the endless
photos that lined every available space, and the complete and utter lack of the recent presence of a vacuum
cleaner.

'I've been home.' When Lydia didn't respond, just
moved a pile of magazines so that he could sit, Anton
elaborated, 'I went to see my family.'

'And Cara?'

'And Cara,' Anton agreed, sitting down in the space
she had cleared. 'What have you been doing since—'

'Working,' Lydia broke in. 'It's busy, as always—I had
a few days off after…' Neither could bring themselves to
say it, the pain of their ordeal still too raw to fully reveal.
'It didn't help. I was just sitting around feeling sorry for
myself, going over and over all that had happened.'

'And all that could have happened?' Anton asked
perceptively, and Lydia knew he wasn't talking about
them, but about the terror of the aftermath—the horrible
tricks one's mind played as it replayed a hundred and
one scenarios. Even if it hurt to see him, would be agony
to say goodbye all over again, for now at least she was
glad that he was here—glad for five minutes in the same
room with the only person on God's earth who truly
knew what she'd been through.

What *they'd* been through.

'I knew that I had to go back to work. Had to get back
on the horse, so to speak.'

'On the horse?'

And somehow, in the most horrible of conversations, they managed a small laugh.

'It's a saying, Anton—the sooner you get back on a horse after a fall…'

'Thank God.' Anton grinned. 'For a minute there I thought you might be in the mounted police. Actually, come to think of it, you'd look good on horseback…' The joking ended then, with a tiny shake of his head to let her know he couldn't make light of it, and his voice was heavier now. 'It's your job.' Anton shrugged, and she was grateful that he didn't pretend to understand, didn't offer her false sympathy.

'It is.'

There was a horrible pause, each waiting for the other to speak. She wished he'd just get it over with—tell her what he'd come for and leave, give her the bad news so she could begin to pick up the pieces and sort out whatever was left of her life.

'You have a nice home.'

God, she hated this stilted, forced attempt at conversation. She almost wished he hadn't come if this was what they were reduced to.

'How's Dario?' She watched as he paled, watched as guilt caught up with him, pathetically grateful that she still had the upper hand.

'Beautiful.' His jaw quilted with emotion. 'Cara showed me some pictures. I have set up a college fund for him…'

'Great!' Lydia didn't even attempt to disguise the bitterness in her voice. 'Just wave your chequebook, Anton, and it will all be fine.'

'Lydia—'

Even the sound of him saying her own name irritated

her now. Furious, she faced him. 'Don't try and justify it to me, Anton. Don't you dare try and justify to me how you could walk out on your own son!'

She'd never expected to reduce him to this—had never thought that she, Lydia, could make this beautiful, vital man literally crumble before her. But that proud, dignified face slipped and the delicious navy eyes filled with tears as he said words that she'd never, even in her most far-fetched of scenarios, contemplated.

Oh, and she *had* contemplated. Tried to fathom reasons, excuses to justify a man walking away from his son—yet however hard she'd tried, still she hadn't quite been able to manage it.

But now, as Anton spoke, he threw every excuse, every reason she'd concocted in his favour on those long, lonely nights into a heap as he admitted his agony.

'He isn't my son.'

And such was the pain behind the simple sentence that in that instant she believed him—knew from the abject agony on his face that this wasn't a lie. She had interviewed too many witnesses, seen too much raw emotion in her time. And if it had taught her one thing, it was to recognise the truth when it finally came.

Lies were complicated, sinister. They slipped off a guilty tongue in defiance and were delivered with tears that beggared belief. But the truth, when it really hurt, was always so much harder to reveal.

'That's why I didn't want Rico to pick up the telephone—why I told him to listen to me instead of you. I knew if Cara revealed the truth to him he'd really go crazy, that it would be the end for us both.'

She sank to her knees and held his hands as he told

her the appalling tale, and knew way beyond the reason-
able doubt she normally lived by that these raw, anguished words came right from his soul.

'I thought Dario was my son. I thought he was
mine…' Navy eyes met hers. 'She let me love him as if
he were my own—and I did love him, Lydia. I loved him
more than I thought it possible to love another…' His
face twisted in pain, balled fists ramming into his
temples as he revisited his private agony.

She didn't know what to say. Truly didn't know
what paltry words she could offer in the face of such
painful truth.

'Nearly two years ago I found myself with four
weeks off work.' Anton's voice was distant, almost void
of emotion now, but his body was rigid beneath her
touch. 'I never get four weeks off—*never,*' he added, just
to make sure Lydia understood the rarity of it. 'But a trip
to the States was suddenly cancelled, and a hotel I had
been considering buying was sold from under my nose,
and suddenly I had four weeks rubbed out of my diary.
So I decided to go home. Even though I live in Italy, I
rarely get back to my village—something I always feel
guilty about—so I decided to take the time and use it
wisely, to catch up on my family.'

She felt his shoulders relax a touch, saw his face soften
as for a second he was back there, back at the beginning
of the dream before it had turned into a nightmare.

'My mother is brilliant at two things: cooking and
talking—and believe me, Lydia, that is not a sexist
comment. She is amazing at both! It took about a week
of solid eating and talking just to bring me fully up to
date on our family, and gradually things moved on to

friends. She told me about a family in the village. The elder brother was in hospital with mental health problems. They needed money for his treatment, but the family were too embarrassed to ask for help.'

'Rico?'

Anton nodded. 'There was a clinic in Florence that the doctors thought might be able to help him, but the family didn't have any health insurance, and the cost of relocating him there would have been too much for them. I went round to see what I could do. They were family friends of my mother, and she told me how good they had been to her during difficult times…' His voice faded to a whisper. 'That is when I met Cara—she was Rico's younger sister, and I guess we…'

'Fell in love?' Lydia finished for him, hating the jealousy those words flared within her. But as Anton shook his head she felt as if a knife was being pulled from her side.

'That happened two years later,' Anton said softly. 'Love came to me when you did.'

It was the most beautiful thing anyone had said to her, but there was no time to dwell on it. It didn't answer the questions that buzzed in her brain.

'It was nice. For three weeks we were together, but it was never going to go anywhere. Cara never wanted to leave, and in truth I didn't want to stay, but for a short time it was special.'

'She got pregnant?'

Anton nodded. 'I didn't know. We didn't keep in touch or anything. But months later she called me, said that she'd been working up the courage to tell me. She'd concealed the pregnancy but now it was out in the open and her family was furious—mine too. I flew home straight away. I told her I would stand by her, that we would be married before the baby was born…'

'You married her?'

'No.' Anton shook his head. 'The baby came prematurely, a few days later, before we'd had time to arrange things.'

'But you would have married her.' Lydia frowned. 'Even though you didn't love her?'

'I cared for her, and believed she was carrying my child.' Anton made it sound that simple—and maybe it was. 'People have married for less. But it never got to that.' She could feel the tension in his body, looked down at his clenched fists as he relived his tale. 'Cara was rushed into Theatre. The baby was tiny, so tiny, and yet my lawyer was telling me he was big—too big to be my baby. He told me to ask for a DNA test.'

'Did you take one?'

Anton shook his head. 'I thought there was no need. I knew he was mine. I trusted Cara. I believed every word she was telling me.'

'She was lying,' Lydia said, and it wasn't a question, just a sad, sad statement. And as Anton gave a slow, leaden nod, in that moment all Lydia could feel was hatred. Hatred for a woman she had never met, for the agony her deceit had caused.

'Dario got sicker. He had been in Intensive Care since he was born, and when he was four weeks old he needed an urgent transfusion in the middle of the night. He has a rare blood group, and because Cara's type was different the pathologist told me that mine would be suitable. He took my blood and said that he would rush through all the tests, that the blood would be ready soon—that it was quicker this way than waiting for it to be flown in. We waited for that blood for hours.' Anton's face was pale beneath his suntan, and there were black rings around his eyes as he forced himself to go on. 'I didn't match. I can still remember the pathologist sitting with me, telling me that there was no way I could help Dario because he wasn't my son.'

A hundred emotions, words, tumbled in her mind as she tried to imagine his horror, his devastation, tried to comprehend what he had been through.

'I confronted Cara and it all came out. Apparently she'd had a brief fling before we met, with a married man in the village; she knew there was a chance the baby was his, but it was easier to say the baby was mine.'

'Easier for who?' Lydia flared, but when Anton just shook his head she knew she didn't really understand.

'For everyone. If the truth had come out she would have broken up a respectable family, her own family's name would have been shamed...'

'So she shamed you instead?'

'I offered because I could take it.' Anton swallowed hard, all the lies, however well meant at the time, finally catching up with him. 'I told Cara she could say I had said I wasn't ready for fatherhood, that I didn't want to be tied down, but that I'd given her money to support Dario.'

'Why?' Lydia begged. 'Why would you say such a thing after all she'd done to you? After all the lies?'

'Because even if I was able to walk away from Cara, I couldn't bring myself to just walk away from Dario. I had to be sure he was going to be okay. That is why I gave her money—so she could provide for him.'

'He's not your responsibility,' Lydia argued, but even as she said them she knew the futility of her words—knew that when a man like Anton loved, he loved for ever.

'I held him, Lydia. I cut his cord when he was born. Even if he is not mine he will always matter to me.'

'And Cara?' God, it hurt to ask—hurt almost more than she could bear. But Lydia needed answers.

'We have made our peace,' Anton said softly. 'The anger is gone now. She was scared; she didn't know what else to do…'

'So she tried to con you!' Lydia retorted. 'I'm sorry.' Pulling her hands away, she stood up. 'It's not for me to judge, and I'm glad you've made up…' She forced a smile. 'I hope you'll both be happy.'

'Both?' Anton frowned.

'All three of you, then,' Lydia snapped, wishing he would just leave, wishing this torturous agony would soon end so that she could give in to the tears that were appallingly close.

'Why would I want to be with Cara?' He sounded genuinely bemused. 'Why do you think—?'

'You said you'd made your peace.'

'It doesn't mean I slept with her.' He was back in control now, his flip response more the Anton of old. 'Lydia, why do you think I am here?'

'I don't know.' Her hands flailed in the air. 'To "make your peace" with me, perhaps? Well, save your breath, Anton. I'm doing fine.'

'Are you?' Gripping her wrists, he stared down at her, taking in a face that was way too pale, way too thin, watching those once confident eyes darting nervously, appalled at the fragility beneath his fingers. 'Lydia, why do you think I left?'

Hadn't he humiliated her enough? Tears filled her eyes and she gave an ungracious sniff as she struggled to hold them back, refusing to cry in front of him—there would be plenty of time for that later.

When she didn't answer, when the words strangled in her throat, Anton spoke for her. 'I left for you, Lydia.' He watched a tiny frown pucker her taut face. 'I left because that day I felt real fear and I truly thought that I couldn't do it—thought that I couldn't be the man you wanted me to be. And I knew if I stayed a moment longer I would try to dissuade you, would beg you to give up your work, and I also needed to talk to my mother about Cara, to explain things face to face...'

'That was the unfinished business?' Wide-eyed, she stared back at him. 'I thought you meant you were going to see Cara.'

'I had to deal with that too. But it is really finished now. Things are better now they are out in the open,' Anton explained. 'Rico is having the treatment he needs, and our families finally know the truth—or most of it.'

'Most of it?'

'I didn't slip in the bit about emigrating, and taking over our Australian franchise. My mother's heart isn't quite what it used to be.'

'Emigrating?' The frown on her face deepened as she whispered the word back to him.

Anton continued—because Lydia couldn't. 'And I admit I omitted to tell her that my future wife is an inspector in the police...' Registering her confusion, he ignored the issues he'd raised and focussed on the one

that really mattered. Cupping her fragile face in his
hands, all joking and flip comments over now, he bared
his very soul. 'I thought I couldn't do it, Lydia. Couldn't
imagine, after all we'd gone through, ever being able to
wave you to off to work, ever allowing you…' His translation skills stalled and she watched as his mind raced
to find the right words. He settled for, '…to be you,' and
it worked beautifully. Tears spilled from her eyes un-
checked now as Anton Santini opened the door to his
heart and invited her to step inside.

'These past weeks I have worked on myself—does
that make sense?'

It made perfect sense. Because she'd worked on herself too. Had spent sleepless nights facing the bigger
issues, had grown up more in these past six weeks than
she had in her entire life.

'At first I thought it was pride—what sort of man
would I be, allowing my wife to do such work?—and
maybe that was a factor. But not now.'

His hands still cradled her face, the nub of his thumb
hushing her as she opened her lips to speak, to reassure
him that finally she understood, that she knew exactly
how he was feeling. But it wasn't that that silenced her.
Instead it was respect and need—respect for his heartfelt words that deserved an audience, and a need to
know how he really felt.

'I couldn't bear the thought of losing you, Lydia. I
couldn't bear the thought of some bastard doing to you
what Rico did—and maybe far, far worse. I almost
managed to convince myself that it would be easier to
walk away, to let you live the life you want and I would
live mine. It took me six damned weeks to realise why

it hurt so much. Six long weeks to work out why I was still in so much pain—because in walking away I'd made my own worst fear come true. Either way, I had losed you.'

'Lost me,' Lydia corrected, but, seeing the pain flicker on his face, she begged an explanation. 'Either way you had *lost* me.' A gurgle of laughter spilled from her lips, in contrast to the tears streaming down her face. 'I was correcting your English, Anton, not telling you it's over. You could never lose me—never in a million years. Because as long as I'm breathing I'm going to love you.'

'You mean it?'

Hope flared in his eyes and his mouth searched for hers, but Lydia pulled away. They had their whole life ahead of them. Kissing, loving, sharing could all come later. Some things needed to be said, and it was Anton's turn to listen.

'You don't have to tell your mum about me being an inspector—'

'I want to be honest now,' Anton broke in.

'So do I.' Lydia nodded, but changed midway, shaking her head against the hands that still held her face. 'I can't do it any more, Anton. I've lost my nerve.'

'You'll get it back,' he said assuredly. 'It will just take time. In a few weeks you'll be back to normal, kicking arse...'

Lydia could scarcely believe what she was hearing— here was the man who hated her job more than anyone encouraging her, almost pleading with her to go back.

'I understand.' Lydia silenced him with two tender words. 'I understand how you feel because I feel it too.

I understand that when you love someone, when you care about someone more than you care about yourself, all you want to do is protect them.' Trembling hands met his, guiding them from her face to her stomach, and she watched in silence as the news filtered through.

'A baby?' His voice was incredulous as the warmth of his hands seeped through her flimsy top, radiating love to the tiny life within.

'Our baby,' she affirmed. 'I didn't take the promotion, Anton. I couldn't. When there was only me to worry about I could take the risks, but not now. I understand how you feel…' Lydia whispered, closing her eyes as his lips met hers, closing the door on the horrors that were behind them, glimpsing a beautiful future ahead.

With Anton protecting them both.

EPILOGUE

'LYDIA!' Anton's urgent voice had her running. Taking the steps of their smart Melbourne home two at a time, she raced into the living room, preparing herself for any appalling eventuality, skidding to a halt as a smiling face greeted hers.

'I think Alexandra has a tooth.'

'It's milk,' Lydia said in a matter-of-fact voice, peering into her eight-week-old daughter's gummy mouth.

'It's a tooth,' Anton insisted.

'It's *regurgitated* milk,' Lydia said, wiping away the offending dot to confirm her point, smiling as she did so. The innocent, never-ending smiles from her tiny daughter never ceased to move her.

Or Anton.

He was as proud of Alexandra as he was dedicated to her—bathing her, singing tunelessly to her, changing the most vile of diapers with barely a word of protest. The only concession to his abhorrent wealth was a night-time nanny.

From seven through to seven it was just about them.

Apart from many final kisses goodnight.

Apart from the night feeds.

Apart from the times Anton nudged her in the ribs when Alex's piercing screams filtered through to their bedroom around three a.m.

Over and over he loved them—loved the two redheaded women in his life; again and again he surprised her.

She'd handed him an envelope ten days after their daughter's birth, because given what he'd been through he deserved it. She'd handed him the irrefutable proof that confirmed that Alexandra was 99.99 per cent his, and he'd handed it back unopened.

No proof of identity needed when none was required.

Trust was easy to achieve with love on their side.

'We're lucky.'

'Very,' Lydia agreed, snuggling into the sofa beside him, watching as he fed a greedy Alex the last remains of her bottle.

'Some children aren't.' Anton gave a rather too dramatic sigh—the sort of sigh that had Lydia frowning; the sort of sigh that had her senses on high alert. 'Don't you wish you could help them?'

'Who?'

'I don't know.' Anton shrugged, way too nonchalantly. 'Kids that maybe have been abused, babies that have no voice…'

Which wasn't exactly idle conversation—wasn't the type of thing Anton usually said at all. In an instant Lydia had worked him out—Anton hadn't developed a social conscience all of a sudden, he'd been snooping where he shouldn't.

'You've been reading my e-mails!' Appalled, she confronted him. 'Don't try and lie to me, Anton— you've been reading my mail.'

'I read one e-mail,' Anton retorted. 'By complete accident.'

'Please!' Lydia snorted, two spots of colour flaming on her cheeks. Because even though she was in the right, even though she had every right to privacy, for some reason she felt as if she'd just been caught with her hand in the cookie jar, felt horribly guilty for not telling Anton what had been going on in her head for the last two days.

'Is there anything you want to tell me?'

'I've been offered a job. Well, I've been invited to apply for a job.' Lydia gulped, staring at her divine daughter and wondering how she could even contemplate leaving her, wondering how she could bear to think about going back to work so soon. 'Kevin phoned me a couple of days ago to see if I was interested, then e-mailed me the job description. It's only part-time.' Lydia breathed through it, bracing herself for his reaction. 'I wouldn't be starting for a couple of months yet. It's as an inspector on the Child Protection Unit.'

'You need to work, don't you?' Anton smiled, and for the thousandth time she was taken aback by his insight.

'I do,' Lydia admitted. 'I guess I must need a bit of guilt back in my life…' Seeing Anton's frown, she elaborated. 'It's no fun buying shoes when you don't need to hide the receipt.'

'Why would you want to hide the receipt?' Anton asked, clearly bemused.

'It's a girl thing,' Lydia said airily. 'We like to feel as if we're doing something we shouldn't.' But her voice changed as she answered seriously the issues going back to work raised. 'I feel awful even thinking about leaving Alex. But, Anton, it's a great job—and it's a lot safer than what I was doing before.'

'No guns?' Anton checked, and Lydia nodded. Then she gave a tiny, hesitant wince.

'Not like before, Anton. But there probably will be a few situations where guns will be present—you've seen the news, you know what goes on. But I'm not going to be armed.'

'It could still be dangerous.'

'Of course it could,' Lydia agreed. 'But it's probably one of the safer jobs that still manages to interest me, and at the end of the day…'

'Don't tell me again how you could get run over by a bus.' Anton gave a tight smile, but his mind was clearly elsewhere. He stared at his gorgeous daughter for an age, before turning to her mother. 'And you need it?' Anton asked. 'You need to work?'

'I do,' Lydia admitted. And it didn't feel wrong saying it but it didn't feel right either. It just…

…was.

'But I can't do it without you fully behind me, Anton. You have to know that there will be sacrifices, that even though the job's part-time I might be late home sometimes. I might have to stay—'

'I do work too,' Anton broke in, and Lydia braced herself, sure that he was about to point out how important his work was, how much more he earned, how he wanted his wife home for dinner. But, as always, Anton surprised her. His next comment told her that he genuinely seemed to understand the problems she might face. 'I do know that it's not always easy to just get away. You don't have to justify that to me.'

'I *know* we don't need the money, and I *know* that there will be days I hate my job more than anything in the world. But that won't mean I want you telling me to leave it, that we don't really need me to be there…' Her voice faded and she stared at his strong, handsome face, listening to the contented sounds from a dozing Alex and wondering for the millionth time how she'd ever got so lucky.

'Go for it, then.' Anton smiled, snapping her out of her trance and back to beautiful reality.

'You're sure?'

'I'm sure.' Anton nodded, but a tiny frown puckered his brow, his face clouding over as he conjured up one horrible prospect. 'On one condition.'

'What?' Lydia was frowning now too.

'No night duty.'

'No night duty!' Lydia cried, rolling her eyes at the appalling concession he was forcing her to make, trying not to over-act too much, but hard pushed to keep the smile off her face. 'Well…' she gave a dramatic sigh '…I suppose if that's what it takes to go back to work…'

'That's what it takes,' Anton insisted, pretending not to notice as Lydia shared a conspiratorial smile with her gorgeous daughter.

'Then I guess that's how it will have to be.'

'Nights,' Anton said, putting Alex in her crib and joining Lydia on the sofa, pulling her close and taking her in his arms, 'are for you and I.'

THREE MORE FREE BOOKS!

This September, purchase 6 Harlequin Presents books and get these THREE books for FREE!

IN THE BANKER'S BED
by Cathy Williams

CITY CINDERELLA
by Catherine George

AT THE PLAYBOY'S PLEASURE
by Kim Lawrence

To receive the THREE FREE BOOKS above, please send us 6 (six) proofs of purchase from Harlequin Presents books to the addresses below.

In the U.S.:	In Canada:
Presents Free Book Offer	Presents Free Book Offer
P.O. Box 9057	P.O. Box 622
Buffalo, NY	Fort Erie, ON
14269-9057	L2A 5X3

- -

Name (PLEASE PRINT)

Address   Apt. #

City   State/Prov.   Zip/Postal Code

098 KKL DXJP

To receive your THREE FREE BOOKS (Retail value: $13.50 U.S./$15.75 CAN.) complete the above form. Mail it to us with 6 (six) proofs of purchase, which can be found in all Harlequin Presents books in September 2006. Requests must be postmarked no later than October 31, 2006. Please allow 4–6 weeks for delivery. Offer valid in Canada and the U.S. only. While quantities last. Offer limited to one per household.

> Presents
> Free Book
> Offer
> PROOF OF
> PURCHASE
> HPPOPSEP06

www.eHarlequin.com